The Forgotten Cemetery
Michael Gregory II

MG Books

Copyright © 2025 by Michael Gregory II

All rights reserved. Printed in the United States of America. No part of this book may be used or reproduced in any manner whatsoever without written permission except in the case of brief quotations embodied in critical articles or reviews.

This book is a work of fiction. Names, characters, businesses, organizations, places, events and incidents either are the product of the author's imagination or are used fictitiously. Any resemblance to actual persons, living or dead, events, or locales is entirely coincidental.

Cover designed by GetCovers.com

Edited by: Tasha Schiedel

For information contact :

mikegreg85@outlook.com

http://www.MG-Books.com

First Edition: February 2025

10 9 8 7 6 5 4 3 2 1

Acknowledgements

This story is loosely based on true events and locations from my younger years.

I'd love to hear if you can determine which parts are based on my experiences.

I want to give a shoutout to my friend Dustin Nelson! Forever supportive since the first grade and has now become a character in my book.

Contents

Prologue		1
1.	Chapter 1	3
2.	Chapter 2	15
3.	Chapter 3	26
4.	Chapter 4	40
5.	Chapter 5	53
6.	Chapter 6	72
7.	Chapter 7	82
8.	Chapter 8	91
9.	Chapter 9	100
10.	Chapter 10	114
11.	Chapter 11	133
12.	Chapter 12	149
13.	Chapter 13	159
14.	Chapter 14	176
15.	Chapter 15	197

16. Chapter 16	208
17. Chapter 17	214
18. Chapter18	235
19. Chapter 19	251
20. Chapter 20	258
Also by	261
About the author	262

Prologue

There is an old cemetery hidden within a town, almost in plain sight, but is easily missed if you don't look carefully. It is a cemetery from the original settlers of the town. Made in the 1800s, but not well kept. It's run down and seems to be forgotten. This land of bones holds many secrets, things happen here that cannot be explained. It is often explored by the teenagers and young adults of the town looking for some form of excitement. Often, these thrill seekers are intoxicated and wind up with more than what they bargained for.

This is a proud town. One that likes to keep its tragedies and traumatic events hidden from all the surrounding cities. Being a small city in Southern California in Los Angeles County, there are plenty of misfortunes that happen within the near vicinity that things can stay hidden and overlooked. What most don't know, is that there are more things that happen within this cemetery than the city police would like to admit.

A group of friends are going to find out about the many disturbing truths that lie hidden within their city. Things that are not of this world. They will find out that the campfire stories that were told to spook everyone were real. Except, the truth is actually much worse. This group of friends will soon realize their love of what they call "ghost hunting" made them stumble upon something that they wish they never had. That is the Pioneer Cemetery.

Chapter 1

Growing up in the small town of Glendora can be boring. So, naturally, Joey, Katrina, and their friends have a tendency of getting up to mischief. There is only a certain level of boredom that a group of nineteen-year-olds can withstand. The only difference is that this group has a morbid fascination with things like horror movies, metal music, and anything that would scare the shit out of most people. Only being a year out of high school, they had part time jobs, which led to many hours of fucking around. None of the group has started college, or even thought about attending for that matter. They were just happy to be free of going to school and having more time to hang out and party.

Like most nineteen-year-olds, Joey lived at home with his parents and older brother, Frank.

Right after graduating high school, Joey decided to turn the family garage into a room where he could party it up at night and not disturb the rest of his family. The garage was transformed into what would be considered the ultimate hang out spot; basically the size of a studio apartment. Fully equipped with all the necessities that these party animals would need. Complete with a refrigerator, a dart board, pool table, couches, along with a small card table. There was a nice big TV with a surround sound system, along with horror movie posters all over the walls. Scream, Texas Chainsaw Massacre, Halloween, to Friday the 13th, all the classic slashers encased and presented with the feel of a movie theatre. There was also a blacklight switch in case they felt like changing up the vibe of the night. The walls were outfitted with insolation in hopes to sound-proof the room. Occasionally they got loud blasting movies or music while being heavily intoxicated with alcohol, weed—or both. Joey's girlfriend, Katrina, basically moved in with him in the garage. It wasn't official that she lived there, but she was never *not* there. Almost every night Dustin and Brian would show up to hang out with the couple. There wasn't much to do in this town, so they always would get together and try to figure out some sort of plan to try and kill their boredom. This usually resulted in a long night of drinking, smoking, watching movies or listening to music.

On one random night, Joey was feeling extra bored. Not really feeling up to doing the same thing they do every night, already drunk, Joey stood up and said, "This is fucking boring. We have only changed the boredom of doing nothing, to doing the same exact shit every single night."

Brian looked at him and responded, "Ok fuck face, what's your bright idea of what we should do then?"

Joey angrily turned his head to look at Brian, "If you would just shut up and listen, I would tell you, you impatient fuck. Let's start ghost hunting. We all love scary things. We love horror movies. We like to read scary books. Halloween is our favorite holiday. Why not try to find the actual scary ass shit that we love so much? What do you guys say? Let's start making trips that are going to give us the chills. Places where we can have adventure. Katrina? Dustin? What do you think?"

Katrina turned to Joey with a big grin on her face, "Hell yea baby, let's do it. I am always up for an adventure."

Dustin turned his head side to side looking at everyone with that weird smile he does. He almost looks like the Cheshire Cat, only he doesn't say anything.

Joey looks at Dustin, "Dustin you weird fuck, you need to actually give an answer, not just one of the weird faces you make."

Dustin, still with the weird smile, jumps up and yells in a strange sounding tone, "Haaaaam-mmmmmmmmm." Then sat down and proceeded to just laugh really hard until he was wheezing.

"Ok... I will just take that as you are game," Joey said, kind of confused. "Brian, looks like you are the last to answer. What do you think? Do you want to do this or what?"

Brian just looks around the room and says confidently, "Of course I am down for that. I live for things like that. When do we start?"

So, it was at this moment the group decided they were going to become ghost hunters. Not like the silly show that is on TV. They want to find real ghosts. Not just find sounds or have little jump scares from the wind blowing. They wanted to see how far they could push the limits. They wanted to find the real scary stuff. They also wanted to be respectful of the dead. They didn't want to disturb the spirits they might encounter. It was Joey's idea, so Joey decided it was probably a good idea if they started researching things the best they could to try to figure out how they could go about this.

Joey knew Katrina was great at researching things, so he pointed her in the direction of trying to figure out how to respectfully communicate with spirits and if there were any specific items they should bring to be safe. Joey, Dustin, and Brian would each try to find different haunted destinations.

"Fuck yea guys, we need to celebrate tonight. This is going to be an awesome adventure we are going to partake in. Maybe one day they will make a movie or write a book about the things we witness. Brian, check the fridge. Is there any more beer in there?" said Joey.

"Nope, fresh out. It's only 11:30 so AMPM still sells beer. Let's go get some. Besides, I think Boss is working so you know he won't check our ID."

"You and Dustin go pick it up then. I bought the last twenty-four pack, it's your turn."

"Fine, I guess we will leave you two to have some alone time for a little bit then. We'll be back, just have your clothes on when we return. Well, only you need to have your clothes on Joey."

Katrina glared at Brian and grabbed a pillow from the couch and threw it at his face. Katrina seems to always have good aim and abnormal strength when she wants to inflict damage on someone. "Go get the damn beer you pervert."

Brian and Dustin proceed to leave on their mission for more alcoholic beverages to ensure they have a grand ole' time celebrating the groups' new purpose of existence–well at least for the time being.

Joey turns towards Katrina, "Sooooooo, what do you think really? This is going to be fun, huh? Let's try to find some scary ass places. Let's have some real adventure."

"It sounds fun, but it also sounds scary Joey. I just hope I can figure out a way to safely communicate or whatever."

"It is supposed to be scary; this is going to be fucking fun. I am telling you, we are going to have the times of our lives doing this."

"You're right, I just get scared of these things you know?"

"Of course I know. I am your boyfriend after all. Don't worry, I will protect you."

Joey then leaned in to kiss Katrina and stood up and picked her up as well and she wrapped her legs around him. Katrina then dropped her legs down and walked off to grab the auxiliary cable to hook up her phone. She then puts on some poppy dance music and starts dancing seductively.

"God damn you are too sexy Katrina," said Joey.

As she continued to dance around, she slowly removed her top. Right as she threw it at Joey the door opened. Brian and Dustin walked in.

Brian said, "All right! I knew we would walk in on some action."

Katrina walked over to Brian and smacked his face, then grabbed two beers from him. She walked over to the couch where Joey was sitting and handed him one.

She looked to Brian and said, "You act like you've never seen a girl in a bra before. It's the same thing as a bikini top. Oh wait, you probably never have seen a girl in person wearing either. You probably creep them all out before that could ever happen."

Joey, Katrina, and Dustin all laugh uncontrollably.

Brian angrily says, "Whatever. Say what you want, but I've had girls before."

"Relax big baby, you don't need to be so defensive." Katrina said in a mocking tone.

Joey stands up and says, "All right, let's celebrate. Let's get drunk and watch a horror movie for inspiration. Obviously, something to do with ghosts." Joey starts looking at his DVD collection. "Let's see, *Thirteen Ghost's*. No, not the vibe I am going for. *1408*, no not that one either. I got it, let's watch a classic. How about *The Shining*? Everyone good with that?"

Katrina gets up and says, "No, I know just the movie watch. It will be fun for the idea of it all. Let's watch *The Sixth Sense*."

The guys look at each other and shrug and nod their heads. Katrina then puts the movie on while they all sit down and watch it. Although they have all seen it many times, no one dares disagree with Katrina when she has her mind made up on what she wants to do. Besides, it does seem kind of fitting. They plan on seeing ghosts, they plan on experiencing entities that are still stuck on this plane of existence. They have high hopes in being able to witness what only some people have supposedly seen. Adventure is what they want, and adventure is what they are going to get, at all costs.

Two hours later and the movie is over. The group are just sitting in their seats, all enjoyably intoxicated at this point. Dustin and Brian have turned their chairs to face Joey and Katrina. Even though they are facing each other, no one is making eye contact. They are just looking towards the ground. Contemplating their decision to be ghost hunters. Wondering if this is a good idea. Everyone's ego at this point is too strong to dare let them even admit any type of fear. It is definitely there, lingering and residing in everyone.

Dustin is the first to break the silence and says enthusiastically, "Well mother fuckers. Are we going to figure out where we are going to go find some mother fucking ghosts? Or are you mother fuckers going to just be mother fucks?"

Joey chuckled thinking about what Dustin just said and responded, "Dustin, sometimes I wonder what the fuck goes on through your mind. You say some weird ass shit, but it also makes you awesome as well. To answer your question, fuck yea, let's figure out our first spot. Where should we go? Has anyone heard of anywhere near by that could be haunted?"

Brian awkwardly raises his hand like he is waiting to be called on by the teacher. Joey just nods to Brian and shakes his head after. "Ok guys, I just remembered. There's a hotel that is supposed to be haunted just a couple cities over in Monrovia. It's called the Aztec Hotel. I don't know the exact room number, but we should stay the night there in that room. It would be a good start."

Joey replies, "Damn Brian. That actually sounds like a good idea. How did you hear about this?"

"I was bored, scrolling the internet. Somehow ended up on that. Not like I knew I would end up wanting to be a ghost hunter myself."

"Well shit, we lucked out, I guess. At least you were good for something, finally."

"Fuck you, Joey."

"I am sure your hand has that covered already."

Katrina and Dustin start laughing and screaming "Oooooohhhhhhhhhh."

Brian says, "Ok, asshole. Whatever. Anyway, I will find out all the details about it. The room number, and hopefully what happened. You guys figure out all the other stuff."

Remembering their earlier conversation Joey said, "Ok baby, can you try to figure out if there is some sort of protocols or safety matters we should take while doing this?" Katrina nodded. "Dustin, can you...fuck I don't know what you can do. Maybe try to get some booze ready? Oh, I know, figure out if there is some sort of electronic shit we should bring to record. You know, like they do on those TV shows. Video camera, maybe some sort of audio recorder or something. Brian, you already gave yourself a job to do. Me, fuck I don't know what I will do right now. I will figure something out."

All excited, they decided to call it a night. Even though they are too drunk to drive, Dustin and Brian leave anyway. Katrina and Joey are too excited to call it a night. So they continued to drink for a couple more hours while discussing everything to do with ghosts and the spirit realm. The level of uncertainty with what will be their new hobby has them all nervous, but ecstatic to engage in something new.

Something different.

Something unknown.

Something dangerous.

Chapter 2

A few days pass before the group could reconvene. Joey had sent out a group text.

Joey: *Alright boogiemen and boogie woman, let's get together and set our plan for our first hunt. Can everyone come over tomorrow night, 9pm?*

Katrina: *You are too cute Joey. I like that, we are the boogies, not the ghosts.*

Dustin: *Yea I can make it. It's Friday tomorrow so let's get this shindig started!*

Brian: *I think I am going to throw up in my mouth. Don't be all cute with each other in our group chat. This is sacred, so don't ruin it and yea I'll be there.*

Joey: *Party pooper Brian can't stand to see people happy.*

Brian: *Fuck you Joey. No one wants to see lovey dovey shit. We aren't here for that. We are here for ghost hunting.*

Joey: *Don't get your panties in a bunch. Anyway, see you guys tomorrow.*

There is always some sort of argument going on when it comes to Brian. He always tends to get offended–or in other words, always has a stick up his ass. The group still likes to have him around for the fun times. Brian is good at finding fun things to do, you just have to bear with the bitching that goes along with it.

A bit after 5PM Joey arrived at home after work, excited to see Katrina, but also to talk to her about their upcoming excursion. Joey parks his car and leaps out, runs to the door to get into the garage. Swinging the door open and flying in as if he was the Kool-Aid man, he spots Katrina on the couch where she appears to be locked in concentration to her computer. Without hesitation, Joey runs to her and jumps at her with his head landing at her lap and arms wrapping around her body. Because Katrina was so focused on her computer, she didn't even realize what had just happened, and screamed when Joey landed on her. Joey giggled at her squeal, but proceeded to give her kisses all over her face.

"Alright hot stuff, have you found any good info to present to the group tomorrow?" Joey said.

"I have found some things. I am trying to see if I can find the same thing more than once to make sure it's not just being made up by this person. It's a lot harder than you think to find any info on how to treat the spirits that are trapped on earth." Katrina replied.

"I bet. I also know, if anyone can figure it out, you are the person who can do it."

"Thank you, baby."

Katrina and Joey then continue to kiss and run their hands over each other exploring their bodies. One thing led to another, passionate love making ensued shortly after.

"Well, that was some good research, Katrina." Joey said with a big smile on his face.

"Some much needed research," Katrina replied.

"I really would love to hear what you have found though."

"Not yet, I want to get some more info and then I will show everyone at the same time tomorrow."

Joey and Katrina just laid in their bed for a bit enjoying their blissful moment in time together. Shortly after, both of their stomachs started to growl. They definitely worked up an appetite and earned this meal with all of their calories burned.

"Alright, let's get up and get some food. I am starving. What do you feel like eating?" said Joey.

"I know exactly what we can eat. It could be a celebration of us finally going to do something fun for once." Katrina said with a smirk.

"Ouch! Note to self, try to plan more fun things to keep the girlfriend happy. Where are we going to celebrate then?"

"Let's go to *Ye Ole Kings Head* in Santa Monica. We can get some bangers and mash, or fish and chips with some drinks. How does that sound?"

"Fuck it, sounds like a plan. Should we invite the guys to tag along, or do you want to make it a date between us?"

"Just us; we are going to see them tomorrow anyway."

Katrina and Joey hopped out of their bed and quickly threw their clothes on to dash out of the room and hit the road. It was going to take a while to get to their destination, so they didn't care how their clothes looked, they could always adjust in the car ride.

******

Dustin and Brian were hanging out together while Brian was trying to research what info he could find for the Aztec Hotel. Brian especially wanted to find lots of information about the hotel to wow his friends. He has a problem of always wanting to show up people, or prove that he knows best. He has what some people would call a superiority complex. Dustin was just hanging out in his room while Brian was searching on the computer.

"Have you found anything worthwhile?" said Dustin.

"Oh yea, I have found some pretty good stuff. I don't want to tell you any of it though. I want to wait so I can show it to everyone at the same time. I gotta make sure I wow you at the same time as the others. This place was my idea after all." said Brian.

"Oh Brian, always trying to one up everyone and show off. It's cool, I like the anticipation. I plan on getting us some good ass drinks. I am thinking some rum and mix it with some root beer. *Barq's* of course. Baaarrrrrkkkkkkkkk. Ha ha ha."

"Dustin, I mean this with all sincerity, you are fucking weird."

"Thank you. I will probably get some beers and maybe something else as well."

"Dude, this is going to be fucking fun. Do you think we might actually see some sort of ghost or something might happen?"

"Fuck, I don't know. I hope so. Regardless if we do or don't, we will probably be hammered. So it's going to be fun as fuck anyway."

"True. I just hope we find something crazy. Oh yea, did you figure out what to bring for recording stuff?"

"I figure I will bring a video camera. Or maybe a couple of them. I have, like, two I can borrow and one tape recorder for standalone audio. Shit, I should've been an asshole like you and not tell you till tomorrow. Oh well. Bitch."

Dustin left a little while later to go home and get some rest for the next day. Brian stayed up for a while still looking into the hotel. He was so excited that he was having trouble going to sleep in anticipation of what may become his new obsession.

******

Friday night, before Dustin and Brian showed up, Joey and Katrina were excited to start planning. Everyone is more excited than they expected to be. Joey had brought out some snacks: chips and dip, as well as cheese and crackers. Katrina also ordered some pizza for everyone. Meat lovers, Hawaiian, and just pepperoni. They also had ordered a side of BBQ wings. Joey looked around the table and realized they probably ordered too much food but could just blame it on the anticipation. Besides, they could always just save it for another night if they don't finish it.

Joey is walking around the room, not able to sit down from being so excited. Joey then checked the fridge for the third time to make sure there were some nice cold drinks for when everyone was there. Only beer and sparkling water in the fridge. It was completely full, so Katrina kept wondering why Joey kept checking. She just put it up to that Joey was probably nervous and was finding something to do.

Dustin and Brian had carpooled together, so they arrived at the same time. Dustin and Brian had walked into the room when they noticed all of the food set up and got excited.

"Hell yea! I'm starving; you guys are the best," said Dustin.

"Is there any beer?" Brian grumbled.

"Of course there is beer. What's up your ass?" Joey said.

"I have had a long day and was up all night. Sorry, I won't be a party pooper," Brian said in a normal tone. They all gathered their plates and drinks and sat down in their normal spots they usually sit. You would think this was assigned seating; they never sit in another spot. They commenced their eating and decided they didn't want to discuss their meeting until after everyone was full and finished their meal.

"Everyone good? Nice and full? Ready to sit back and relax, while figuring out how awesome this is going to be?" Joey said enthusiastically.

Everyone nodded with a smile. "Perfect. First let's take it to you Brian. I want to hear what you got about the place," Joey continued.

"Ok, check this shit out guys. First of all, there has been many ghost sightings at this hotel. It was built in 1924 and was very popular back in the day. There are two rooms specifically that are known to have the most activity. The first one being #120. It is supposedly haunted by a girl who was killed on her wedding night. She was said to have been shoved and hit her head on the radiator in the room. I figured Joey and

Katrina would stay in that one. The other room is #129, so they aren't very far apart. They don't have any known deaths or things that happened there specifically, just that there has been a lot of activity," said Brian.

"First off, fuck you Brian for saying we should stay in the room with the murdered woman on her wedding night. Second, damn you found some good info. Sounds like a plan. Dustin, what do you got for us?" said Joey.

"I was able to get my hands on two video cameras luckily. We can put one in each room. They are not digital cameras so we will have to change the tapes. I will make sure each of us has enough for the first night. I will also make sure we have enough booze for the night too."

"Solid work Dustin. I saved my favorite for last. Katrina, what do you got for us?"

"Damn right I am your favorite," Katrina said and winked at Joey. "So as far as protecting ourselves from evil entities, surrounding ourselves with salt will keep us safe. So, when you're sleeping, just put a circle of salt around the bed or wherever you are sleeping. If you are caught in an area where they are coming at you, or something of the sort, hitting them with iron will send them away. At least for a brief moment. This is all just from lore, so we can hope that it's true. I couldn't really find much else. There isn't really anything to go off of that is more modern. This is all from a long time ago. I figured we can find some scrap iron and cut them into small pieces that we can have on hand just in case."

"Good job baby. It all sounds like we are set. Being I didn't have anything to do, I decided to come up with a nick name for our little group. Let's call ourselves *The Spirit Brigade*. What do you guys think?"

Katrina, "I love it."

Dustin, "Hamtastic."

Brian, "I guess that's alright."

"Brian always has to be negative in one way or another. Glad you guys all like it though. Maybe I will print some t-shirts or something," Joey laughed. "Now that this is all settled, and we are officially official. When are you guys good to go stay there? I will call in for the reservations. What do you guys feel about tomorrow? Are you both off of work?"

"I am good for tomorrow, I have tomorrow off and I don't start on Sunday till 2pm," said Dustin.

"I work tomorrow, but I am off at 3PM, then I am off on Sunday, so that works perfectly," said Brian.

"Sweet, I will call and reserve both rooms. I will let you know if I run into any problems. I will pay for our room, you guys can pay for your room, cool?"

Brian and Dustin both gave a thumbs up. With everyone satisfied with what the plans are, they continued the rest of the night drinking beers and snacking on the food and just like that ,*The Spirit Brigade* was created. Little did they know they were about to embark on many wild adventures.

Chapter 3

The day is finally here, *The Spirit Brigade's* first mission. Saturday afternoon, Katrina and Joey are waiting impatiently in their room pacing back and forth with excitement. Double checking their bags, making sure they have the supplies they wanted to bring. Katrina opens her bag, counts the big containers of salt. Making sure there was at least one per person. Joey was looking at the two foot iron rods he had taken and cut from a fence of an abandoned house down the street.

Joey looked to Katrina and said, "Do you want to take a shot or drink a beer? Calm the nerves a little bit?"

"Yea, ok. How about a shot of vodka?"

Joey knows Katrina likes vodka and brought some anticipating her needing it to calm her nerves.

"Yup, I sure do. It's the only one that I can drink and be normal. You know I get too wild with tequila, whiskey burns, rum, well rum I am ok with, too but I like vodka better."

"Alright, well here's your shot. I enjoy your wildness when you drink tequila though. It usually involves your clothes being anywhere but on you."

"That was one time. I drank a bunch of beers and tequila, and the pool looked amazing. I didn't have a swimsuit and didn't want to get my clothes wet, so skinny dipping seemed like the next best thing."

"Hey, I am not complaining. I don't think anyone else was either. Also, its every time with tequila, not just the one time."

Katrina punched Joey in the arm and rolled her eyes. The door swung open, Dustin and Brian wandered in. Both with giant grins on their faces.

"Hey Brian, I was just reminding Katrina of the time she drank too much tequila and skinny dipped at your party. Remember that?" said Joey.

"How could I forget? That was one of the best sights I've ever seen."

"I wasn't complaining about it either," said Dustin.

Katrina blushed and walked away to go look in her bag so she didn't have to talk to them about her tequila infused antics.

"On second thought, maybe we should drink some tequila. Let's all take some shots of tequila before we head over to the hotel," said Joey.

"Hell yea," said Dustin and Brian simultaneously.

"Oh whatever, why not. We aren't sharing a room with them anyway, so what does it matter if I get naked," said Katrina.

"That's the spirit Katrina," Joey said encouragingly.

They all took a shot or four of tequila. Now that they are starting to get buzzed, they decided this would be a good time to get over to the hotel. If they continued to drink like this, they weren't going to make it to the hotel. Joey drove his car so they could all go together. On the ride there, everyone was starting to feel good. Katrina was sitting in the front seat and started to play some dance music. Katrina started to dance in her seat to the rhythm of *Don't Cha* by *The Pussycat Dolls*. Very fitting, everyone did indeed wish their girlfriend was hot like Katrina.

It did not take a long time to drive to *The Aztec Hotel* in *Monrovia*. They arrived and immediately took all of their bags out of the trunk. They knew it would probably look weird to the person at the front desk, being they were only staying one night and had multiple bags. The clerk did not ask about the bags when they had checked in. They must be used to seeing people come in with equipment or excessive bags, especially when staying in those specific rooms.

Joey and Brian walk away from the front desk counter with big smiles on their faces as they walk back to Katrina and Dustin. Both being as excited as a young child about to run to the Christmas tree on Christmas day. The alcohol didn't help their giddiness.

Giggling, Joey and Brian both said at the same time, "We got the keys."

Katrina sarcastically said, "No shit Sherlock and Watson."

Everyone stopped and looked around at each other for a second, then burst into laughter. The four were a little more buzzed than they expected to be. They were also more anxious.

They didn't know what to expect for their night, so there was a certain level of fear from the uncertainty.

"Let's get all our bags put away and set up our equipment in our rooms. After you guys are done, head over to our room where we can hang out until it's time to try to communicate with the spirits. Cool?" Said Joey.

Dustin and Brian nodded, and they all headed to the stairs to go up to their rooms. Once in their room, Joey and Katrina just paused for a moment to take the place in. They had felt an awe knowing that so many people had stayed in this hotel, shit, how many people had stayed in this room alone. What makes you wonder is, if there is a possibility that many have died in this room. The story only speaks of one murder in this room. But, like most old buildings, there are plenty of deaths that have occurred without being documented. Especially when there were illegal activities going on, like prostitution.

Joey and Katrina had taken out the camera and set it up on the dresser facing towards the room. They had also set up the audio recorder in the bathroom, just in case something could come from over there. Excited, they both looked around and then met each other's gaze. Not saying a word, they both nodded to each other as if they had read each other's mind with a telepathic message. Without hesitation they both walk to the bed, sit down, and open up one of the bags that were on the ground. Joey pulls out the bottle of tequila to take a drink.

Katrina looks at Joey with a devilish grin and grabs the saltshaker and lime juice, the kind of lime juice that looks like a plastic lime with the yellow pop top from the bag. They both take three shots back-to-back as if they were passing a joint back and forth trying to make sure they don't waste any time. After the third shot they set down the bottle, shaker, and juice. Both making scrunched up faces from the sour juice. They lay back and stare up at the ceiling and let out a loud sigh. You would think the two of them were one and the same with how synchronistic they are.

They both look at each other and start to giggle, they slowly start to scoot to each other until their faces meet. Starting to kiss, their hands start to explore each other. Like clockwork, Brian and Dustin knock on their door with an obnoxious loudness. Joey slowly and regrettably gets up to open the door. His friends standing at the door holding two bags full of alcoholic beverages and having devious grins.

"Did we interrupt you two from some private time? I know you were drinking tequila," said Brian in a low voice.

"No fuck face, we were playing monopoly waiting for you. Dumbass. Seriously though, no, we are here for a mission. We are here as a squad, *The Spirit Brigade*. Nothing is going to get in-between me wanting to do this mission to the fullest. Now, let's have some fun and drink some drinks. Eat some good food and snacks. Let's see some ghosts hopefully," said Joey.

Brian and Dustin walked into the room. Katrina was still sitting on the bed leaning back on her elbows.

"What's up boys? Ready to see some crazy stuff happen?" Katrina said with a slur.

"As long as it's not a big barl." Said Dustin.

Everyone just looks at Dustin. After around five seconds they all start laughing.

"What does that mean again?" asked Joey.

"A big hairy fat man."

They all laughed even harder.

"My god Dustin. Some of the shit you come up with," Katrina said while trying to take breaths in-between laughing.

"I can't help it; I was just made this awesome," said Dustin.

The group continued to drink and snack for the next couple of hours. Looking at his watch, Brian notices that it is getting close to 10:30PM.

"Hey, guys. It's 10:30 now. We should try to quiet it down now. Let's keep it down and calm the room and see if we can see the ghostly prostitute visit us."

"You must be really desperate if you want to get a dead prostitute," joked Katrina.

Dustin and Joey erupted with laughter. They both fell off the bed from where they were sitting. Both on the ground convulsing in laughter, even though there was no sound coming from them.

"Holy shit Brian, keep it in your pants. You can't be giving dead dick delivery," said Joey.

Laughter persisted for another five minutes straight.

"You guys are a bunch of assholes," Brian said agitatedly.

For what seemed like forever and a day of them all laughing, they finally calmed down. In reality it was only a few minutes, but it was the longest, funniest three minutes of the night. Settling into the spots they chose to sit; they sat in silence. Looking around, waiting for something, anything to happen. During this waiting period, they continued to drink their drinks. The amount of bathroom trips between them were becoming more frequent. They decided that it has been enough time, only being two hours and getting close to 1:00AM they would just say fuck it and enjoy the night and have a good time. Doing as they would if they were hanging out in the garage, they just conversed and joked while drinking the night away. It was around 2:45AM, Dustin and Brian decided they would head back to their room for the night. It was about time to switch the camera tapes in both rooms anyway.

Dustin gave Joey the new tape to put into the camera for while they were sleeping before leaving the room. Joey put the new tape into the camera then stumbled his way over to the bed and laid down on top of the covers. Katrina was by the dresser where the camera was set. She took a few steps forward, so she was knowingly in front of where it was filming. She started to dance, seductively swinging her hips. Slowly she removed her shirt. She then removed her bra, giving Joey a sexy show. Katrina started to pull her pants down when she stopped, just barely revealing the top part of her thong underwear. Covering her breasts with her right hand she turns around and wiggles her finger at the camera and shaking her head no; Katrina walks to the camera and turns it off.

Joey laughs and says, "You just had to throw that in there didn't you? Make them think you forgot about the camera, just to tease them. That's hilarious. Now finish taking those pants off and make your way over here for real."

"I thought it would be fitting after all the tequila; my clothes never actually came off. So I had to tease them, make them think that they were going to see something good. Enough talk though, time to play," replied Katrina.

Joey and Katrina made the most of their hotel room and made sweet drunk love in every spot they could within the room. When they finished, Katrina passed out in the bed still in her birthday suit. Joey remembered to go back to the camera, not before covering up Katrina and turn it back on so it can record while they sleep.

Joey woke up to knocking on the door when he looked at his watch and saw it was 10:00AM. He walked over to the door and looked through the peephole. It was Brian and Dustin, so he opened the door.

"What's up guys? Did you see anything in your room?" said Joey with a big yawn.

"Nope. Looks like you saw some action though." Brian said while pointing over to Katrina who was laying belly down with the white sheet barely covering her butt.

"Yea, you are definitely right on that one," Joey replied with a big grin. "Hey baby, we got company."

Katrina just turned her head towards the three of them and gave them a thumbs up. Katrina was very comfortable with her body and wasn't very shy. She sat up facing the opposite of the guys in the doorway. Covering up her breasts with one arm and using her other hand to cover her lady bits, she stood up and walked to the bathroom and closed the door.

Brian was speaking and stopped mid-sentence when Joey punched him in the arm.

"Fucking pervert," Joey said jokingly.

"What? I can't help that your girlfriend decided to just up and walk across the room naked. I mean, come on. That just made this whole trip worthwhile," said Brian.

Katrina came back out of the bathroom; this time she was wearing a short silk bathrobe. "Alright boys, put your eyes back in your skull. You are acting like a bunch of teenage virgins who have never seen a set of tits or an ass before. Brian, I don't blame you, I know it's probably true for you."

Katrina just went back to the bed, put the pillow against the headboard, and sat against it while putting her legs atop the bed.

Joey looked back to Brian and Dustin, "We will have to go back to the garage and watch the videos. See if we possibly caught anything on camera that we might've missed. You want to just check out and head back there and get started on that?"

"I am down with the clown to watch this show go down," said Dustin.

"I am down. We can even start the day off with some bloody Mary's or something to kick this hangover," replied Brian.

"Hell yea, let's get some food on the way home too. We can just grab our stuff really quick and be on our way," said Joey.

Joey proceeded to grab all his stuff and throw it into his bags. He put a t-shirt on, then his socks and shoes. He was already wearing some sweat shorts, so he didn't care about putting different pants on. He was finished grabbing all his stuff and looked over to Katrina. She looked over to him and realized everyone was waiting for her to grab her stuff and get dressed so they could leave. She just sighed and put her legs down on the ground. She then grabbed her workout style shorts and slipped them on under the robe. She then dropped the robe and put on a tank top. She grabbed all her things and stuffed them all into her bags and put on her sandals. Ready to go.

Joey walked over to the camera and audio recorder and hit stop for both. Tossed them into one of the bags he was holding, gave the place a double look to make sure they didn't leave anything behind, then proceeded to leave to check out and be on their way home.

Chapter 4

They all arrive at Joey's home at the same time. Eager to go over their recordings, they practically jump out of the cars before they are even fully stopped. Joey and Katrina are carrying all of their bags; Dustin and Brian have their food bag, plus the bag holding the equipment. Dashing into the garage, practically tripping over each other, Katrina was the first one in. Of course, the guys are still gentlemen in the sense they always let the woman go first. She was carrying the food for Joey and her, so she took it over to the table in front of their usual sitting spots.

Joey, Dustin, and Brian all piled in after setting their bags down on the floor. Joey tossed the clothing bags off to the side and grabbed the camera out of the other. He walked over to the TV and connected the AV cables to the camera and TV. Knowing that there is a lot of footage to go through, Joey thought it might be best to watch these at a faster speed.

"Ok everyone, I am going to play this at 1.3 speed so we can get through it faster. Any objections?" said Joey.

"Yea, we won't be able to hear the audio clearly if we do that," replied Brian.

"Good point. I guess we will have to watch these with normal speed and turn the volume way up so we can see if it picks up audio."

Dustin chimed in, "It's now 11:00AM. I can stay for like an hour and a half. I know you guys will probably watch more after I leave. If you find anything, make sure you mark it on a paper with a timestamp or something."

"Will do. Do you guys want to start with your tapes or ours?" Said Joey.

"Let's start with yours. I don't think there was anything in our room," Dustin replied.

Joey responded with a thumbs up. He then proceeded to play the video recording of the first tape of the night. It started off with Joey and Katrina taking shots of tequila sitting on the bed, then as they laid back and started to kiss, Brian said, "Hold on. Pause it here."

"What, why?" said Katrina.

"I need to get some popcorn for this part."

Katrina threw a pillow from the couch at Brian. With perfect accuracy, it hit him in the face while he was taking a drink of beer. He spilled some of the beer on his pants.

"What the fuck? Why did you do that?" said Brian.

"You deserved it," Katrina responded.

"What, you can't take a joke?"

"Oh, you can't take a joke of me play throwing a pillow? Besides, I am just a small girl. Ha ha ha ha ha."

"Damn Brian, for someone who always tries to be so macho you got owned by this 115pound girl."

"You just got hosed bitch. Ha ha ha." yelled Dustin.

"Whatever, can we just get back to the video? You guys are a bunch of assholes."

The video continued to play as it proceeded to the rest of the night's events with all of them in the room. Towards the end of the night, before Dustin and Brian left the room, there was a moment that a bottle moved on the nightstand next to the bed.

Dustin stood up and pointed to the TV, "Oh, did you, that moved. It was, ah, fuck. Tequila."

Joey paused the video, "English Dustin."

"Rewind the video. The tequila bottle moved by itself."

Joey excitedly rewound the video and hit play again. There it was, everyone saw the bottle shift on the nightstand. They all stood up, shocked, and feeling accomplished.

"Fuck yea! Looks like we found something guys," Emphasized Joey. "I hope there is something else on our videos. Who knows, there could be so much else we find. The Spirit Brigade is in business."

Joey walked back to his seat after pacing around for a few moments in exhilaration. The video reached the part of the night when Dustin and Brian depart to their room. Which led to the point of the night where Katrina started to tease the camera.

Brian whistles, "I knew it. I knew the tequila was going to make this video something worthwhile."

Knowing how the rest of the night goes, and that Katrina only teases the camera to shut it off,

Joey was smiling and let out a small chuckle at Brian's remarks.

Brian disappointedly says, "Dammit, I knew it was too good to be true."

The video continues with Katrina asleep in bed and Joey walking back to the bed after starting the camera back again.

Dustin jumps up emphatically, "Shit! I forgot I needed to go to work. I only have a few minutes. Fuck it, I am going to call out and tell them I got a bad case of diarrhea while driving to work and had to stop at a toilet on my way and there was no way I could work."

The group just laughed after Dustin said his plan. They all stayed quiet as he called in and made his performance of having a bad case of diarrhea to his boss while exaggerating the pain of his stomach. He definitely put on a good show for them, one so good that several times they almost erupted into laughter, which only would have derailed his call out. Luckily, they were all able to hold it together.

Dustin hangs up his phone and makes his cheshire cat smile, "Alright mother fuckers. Pass me a beer now. Looks like I'm here for the long haul."

After a few hours of watching Katrina and Joey sleep, the crew decided to take a meal break. They all decided pizza was going to be the perfect pairing for watching their videos; it also helps they deliver. Besides, pizza goes hand in hand with beer. They didn't break out any liquor, they wanted to make sure they were somewhat coherent while watching the videos. They didn't want to get to their usual levels of intoxication and possibly miss something of importance.

The pizza arrived and it was time to get back to watching the tapes. The tedious amount of time left of just watching them sleep was leaving them a little restless. Excited, but alcohol doesn't exactly help their attention spans. The group started to chat more while watching, thus leading to missing the sheet on the bed being moved. The top corner of the sheet was pulled down some, exposing part of Katrinas breast. Surprisingly, no one had noticed even though it had been exposed for several minutes. Katrina had eventually rolled to her side, covering herself up going unseen.

The tape had finally gotten to the morning where they woke up to Dustin and Brian waking them up by knocking on the door. At that point, the rest is history. This had taken up many hours of the night. Now they are all completely inebriated at this point. They figured it would be a good idea for Brian to take the video tape of himself and Dustin sleeping to review. Dustin will take the audio companion for review. Joey and Katrina will get the chance to review the audio of their own room. They decided to re-convene the following day with their findings.

In the meantime, later that night, they started discussing where would be their next visit. Joey had remembered there was a haunted forest in Pasadena. This had sounded like a fun idea to them all. They figured they could all do some research on this forest before meeting back up together and getting more information to share and getting an action plan together while they are at it.

Joey had started to relay some stories that he had heard about the haunted forest. "I heard that when people go there, it feels like someone is watching you. I also heard about people getting the feeling of getting grabbed, even when no-one is around them. Like someone had grabbed them by the wrist or the ankle or some shit like that. I think this will be a big step for us. Maybe we can get some sort of physical contact with a spirit. The only question is, how are we going to get some type of recording of this? The cameras might be too big, or hard to carry around. Unless they have night vision too, it would be pointless, no?"

Dustin says, "Well in this case, we can just use the audio maybe? We can describe what is happening if anything does. I'll look into some sort of night vision camera in the meantime and maybe we can get it before we go."

Joey responds, "Hell yea Dustin. That's what I am talking about. We can all chip in and get a night vision camera. We can wait to get it before we go, too. I mean... if it doesn't take too long to get here at least. What do you think Brian, Katrina?"

Brian just put his hand out balled in a fist, and after waiting three seconds, gave the slow-motion thumbs up with a smile. Katrina smiled widely and shook her head up and down to say yes. At this point, everyone was ready to call it a night. Joey slowly crept into bed waving good night to Brian and Dustin. Katrina started to follow him into bed while starting to toss off her clothes, waiting to get under the covers to remove her undergarments. She also waves bye to their comrades. Dustin and Brian take the hint and wave to them as they walk out the door.

******

The following night the Spirit Brigade has their meeting in session.

"First off, let's go over any findings from the rest of the recordings. We listened to the audio of our room. Really only starting from when we went to bed because it was too loud to hear anything when were all in the room. We only heard some creaking of the bed every now and then. Pretty sure it was just one of us moving around in our sleep. Other than that, quiet," said Joey.

Brian jumped up, "I watched our video very closely. I saw fucking nothing at all."

Dustin yells, "Haaaaaaaa. The audio had absolutely nothing as well."

Katrina shakes her head, "Thanks Dustin. Way to get everyone's hopes up with the enthusiasm and then a great big letdown."

Dustin smiles and gives a little laugh.

"Well, now that that is settled. Let's move on to our next mission. Pasadena haunted forest. I did find some more things online where people shared their experience of feeling like they were grabbed in one way or another. One even claimed to of almost been tripped by whatever grabbed them," Joey said.

Brian says, "Yea I heard basically the same kind of stuff. There seems to be a lot of activity here. I think this was a great find, so props to you Joey. Dustin, did you find out anything about the camera?"

Dustin lifts his head up high, "As a matter of fact mother fuckers. You are going to want to hear what I have to say." Dustin pauses to create anticipation while looking side to side. "I absolutely found a good night vision camera. It's a small one, too. One that you can strap on to your chest with a little harness thing you can buy. Best part, they aren't even that expensive. Like 200 each. So maybe we can each buy one. That way we have multiple angles. Another great thing about it, you can have them shipped to the store for free and usually ships faster there."

Joey responds, "That's fucking great! Let's order them now. Did it give a timeline of how fast the cameras can be shipped to the store?"

"It says anywhere from two to five business days. I looked at the reviews. They said that if you order in Southern California, it's way faster. The manufacturer or whoever ships them out is based in California too so it's much faster."

"Hell yea, alright let's order them and see how long it takes. I guess for now, maybe we should try to find future places to go to while we wait for the cameras. What do you guys think?"

Everyone at this point shook their head saying yes and giving a thumbs up.

"Ok, well that settles it. I guess we will be waiting for the cameras. In the meantime, we can find our next destination for the following outing. Does anyone have any suggestions?"

"Well, when looking at the haunted forest in Pasadena, I did see that there is the bridge to nowhere. That is supposed to be haunted from all the people that have gone there to commit suicide," said Katrina.

"I also had found that The Queen Mary ship in Long Beach is haunted. They do haunted tours there, too," Joey responded.

"Let's not do haunted tours. That seems like it would be too washed down and not let us do any real exploring. The Bridge to Nowhere does sound promising for a future exploration. I just remembered something that I had heard about. This place is actually right in our own town of Glendora. It's called the Pioneer Cemetery. It is the cemetery of all the original settlers in our town. It's hidden, tucked away behind the big nursery by the train tracks. Not only did I hear that it was haunted, I heard there was a cult that lived nearby there. It might be a very scary place to check out," Joey excitedly explained.

"Fuck to the yes," said Dustin. "That sounds like one hell of a mother fuck to go to. I say we go there after we do the haunted forest. Brian? Katrina? What say you?"

Brian shrugs, "Sounds like a winner to me."

Katrina nods, "I guess it's settled. That sounds like a good place to me, too."

Joey smiles, "Good, I am glad you guys thought this would be a good place, too. I almost forgot about it. I had just barely heard about it from someone at work. They said they had a friend that checked it out and was scratched on the back by a ghost. He wasn't with him, but he said he believed his friend. Besides, there were small red scratches on his back when he showed him."

All of the group was excited with anticipation. Not only were they going to be getting new equipment that will give them increased ability to see in the dark when they review their footage, they also have set the next two destinations of their explorations. What started as something to have fun with has now grown into something more. Although they are not sure what it is growing into just yet, they could all feel that this is going to be bigger than what they know it to be.

Chapter 5

A few days pass and the recording equipment has arrived at the store ready for pickup. Dustin had received the notification text and he immediately sent out a group text to let everyone know it was about to be go time.

Dustin: *Alright you sons of bitches. Our cameras have arrived at the landing pod. Touchdown has been achieved. Mission is ready to start.*

Brian: *Did anyone understand that?*

Katrina: *Yea, I got it, cameras are here and we can start the next hunt.*

Joey: *Hell yea. I can't wait to get this shindig started.*

Brian: *Thanks for translating Katrina.*

Katrina: *No problem smart ass.*

Dustin: *Brian = ass of the dumbed.*

Joey: *HAHAHAHAHAHAHA*

Katrina: *Best text yet!*

Brian: *Oh shut the fuck up everyone. Let's just hurry up and get out to this haunted forest.*

Joey: *Can we say backpedal? Alright everyone, let's go in two nights?*

Brian: *Ass. Yes, sounds good.*

Dustin: *Superb.*

Katrina: *You already know I am in.*

It was now set, everyone agreed to go in two days.

*****

It is now the day that they had agreed upon to go and explore the haunted forest. Joey, Dustin, and Brian were at work, but luckily everyone had an early shift. Joey was the first to get off of work. He had hurried home with excitement. As soon as he got home, he had once again ran into the garage busting in faster that he probably should, as if he was the Kool Aid man. Slamming into the door before turning the knob and practically breaking the door down. Katrina was sitting on the couch watching TV, a show called The Ghost Whisperer. Katrina jumped from the loud and abrupt noise from the result of Joey arriving home.

"Jesus Joey! Do you have to run through the door? You could easily just come in like a normal person," said Katrina.

"That would imply that I am a normal person though. If I was a normal person, I would be boring. If I was boring, I probably wouldn't have you. Therefore, the answer is no. I will not be a normal person," replied Joey.

"Well, when you put it that way, I guess I don't mind you being a big loud annoying weirdo."

Joey blows Katrina a kiss and throws his stuff across the room and rips off his clothes until he is in his birthday suit. Without saying anything, he runs to Katrina, jumps on her, gives her a bunch of kisses on her face, slaps her ass, gets up and runs to the bathroom to take a shower. Katrina doesn't even hesitate to continue to watch her show, this is a very typical homecoming of Joey after work.

Joey came out of the bathroom and proceeded to get ready for the events they have planned ahead of their night. He dressed comfortably wearing all black, (which is pretty typical for him anyway) sweatpants for extra covert movement, and a long sleeve shirt. Looking over to Katrina, who was still on the couch watching TV, still wearing brighter colored clothes. Realizing this, Joey thought it would be fun to take matters into his own hands. Joey ran over to Katrina, grabbed her shirt and yanked it over her head faster than she could even recognize what was happening. Just as fast, he grabs her jeans, unbuttoned with one hand and yanked them off of her.

He then threw the clothes across the room. Then simulated to play the bongos on her bare butt. Katrina pushed herself up onto her hands and knees shoving Joey back in a very seductive way. Joey was facing a conundrum, to stay and enjoy his current situation, or to wait till a later time for this extracurricular activity. Joey thought for about two seconds when his body made the decision for him. Like clockwork, as Joey and Katrina were amidst lust and passion, there was a knock on the door. Not willing to be interrupted as they usually are, Joey yells out, "come back in ten minutes. We are not ready yet."

Brian says, "God dammit, you are fucking, aren't you? Of course you are. Whatever, I'll go get some food. Do you want anything?"

Joey yells back breathily, "Yea, just get us what we usually get from wherever you are going. If you don't know, make a wild guess."

Just like that, Brian left to go get food, calling Dustin on his way out. Joey and Katrina could hear Brian on the phone saying, "Hey Dustin, do you want some food? I got here but they are fucking again so I didn't want to wait outside."

They took a break and laughed a little before continuing on with their sensual wrestling match.

*****

Everyone is sitting in their normal spots eating their Del Taco. Dustin is overly excited about giving instruction on how to use the recording equipment. Although it is easy to figure out, they all let him go with it. He was getting very theatrical and reenacting different scenarios. He was jumping up, rolling on the ground, and dashing across the room while saying, "Whoa....ha....heeeeya...ha m....mmmmmbooooowwwweeeeelllllllll." They all started laughing hysterically. Dustin had finally finished his long winded instructional.

Panting and looking around at everyone, Dustin breathlessly said, "Ok....everyone got it?"

Everyone responded in unison, "Yes Dustin, we get it now."

"It is just about go time. Let's pack up the gear, get ready for our first outdoor exploration. And of course we will need to take a mandatory shot. Katrina, grab the tequila and some shot glasses," said Joey.

"No way, not tequila. How about rum? Let's have some rum and root beer. A mixed drink, not a shot," said Katrina.

"Alright, let's do that."

Katrina grabbed and poured the celebratory drinks. After packing up the bags, they all gathered around and picked up their cups.

Joey lifts his cup, "Here's to a hopeful and successful ghost hunt to the haunted forest of Pasadena. Let's make this the best one yet for The Spirit Brigade."

Everyone lifts their cups as well and cheers, "To the Spirit Brigade."

They downed their drinks and walked outside carrying their packs. They brought the essentials: cameras, flashlights, audio recorders, water, and trail mix. It was finally the time they were all waiting for. Time for departure. They all get into Brian's car, he has the biggest and most comfortable car so it only seemed fitting. Brian starts the car, and of course he had the Ghostbusters theme song already queued up waiting to be played.

Off they go on their way to the wonderful city of Pasadena, jumping on to the 210 West Freeway. Being that it is late at night, around 10:00 pm—and also in the middle of the week— there is no-one on the freeway. So that means they can drive a little faster and get to the Haunted Forest quicker. Everyone is full of anxiety, not knowing what to expect. Even though there is loud music playing in the car, there is silence between them all. As they start to approach the exit to Lake Avenue, everyone is getting a little antsy.

To break the uneasy silence, Joey said, "So, looks like we are almost there. Let's have some fun here. Hopefully we can see some cool shit. I hope we don't see anything dangerous while we are at it."

Brian responded nervously, "Fuck yea. I am excited and not scared at all. I hope we see some crazy shit tonight. I hope it is worth the trouble we went through to get here."

Katrina rolled her eyes, "If you have to say you are not scared, you are obviously scared. No matter what happens or doesn't happen, I think the thrill of this all will make it worth it."

Dustin chimes in, "Dumbass Brian trying to be a hard ass and pretend not to be scared at all. If you aren't even a little scared, that means you are a lot of stupid, stupid."

Joey jumps in, "Ok everyone, let's take it easy here. We have some fun times to be had. No matter how dumb or scared Brian is. Let's just have a good time."

Brian starts to say something and looks over at Joey who is just shaking his head as if saying no with a very serious look on his face. Brian just shook his head to himself and kept quiet. They had finally reached the top of Lake Avenue. It is time to park the car on the side of the road and get ready for the adventure.

Brian parks the car, takes out the keys and looks around at everyone. They all open their doors at the same time. Almost as if they had coordinated to open them in unison. Stepping out, Dustin grabs his bag and hands out the cameras for everyone to wear. Equipping themselves with the harnesses and strapping the cameras on the front of their chest, Joey looked at Katrina and giggled.

Katrina noticed his laugh, "What's so funny?"

Joey responds cheekily, "Your camera will be boob-vision."

Joey, Dustin, and Brian laugh harder than they should.

Katrina giggles, "Yea, I suppose you're right."

Cameras on. Audio recorders on and attached to one of the harness straps. One thing that Brian noticed, but for lack of everyone thinking him being a scaredy cat, he didn't mention that there were absolutely no cars here tonight. Most people that have visited the Haunted Forest have usually come in a larger group. At the minimum, there would usually be some other paranormal explorers. For whatever the reason, there is absolutely no one at the trail on this night.

The Spirit Brigade is now ready to start their exploration of Pasadena's Haunted Forest. They all start to walk up the trail, it is a cold, brisk night. This particular part of the trail appears to be getting colder the deeper they get into the trail. Joey takes the lead with everyone else trailing right behind him. They all stop and look around noticing that the trees cover most overhead and it feels as if a chill is running from the top of their neck, down their spine. They all simultaneously shiver.

"Did you feel that?" Joey spun around to look at everyone. "I felt a chill slowly creep down my whole back."

Katrina, Dustin, and Brian all respond at the same time, "I felt the same thing."

Everyone's eyes opened wide realizing they all felt the exact same thing. At that moment, they also realized they could see their breath now that as they were speaking, which was not the case a few moments ago.

"Is it just me or did the weather drop like fifteen degrees in the past five minutes?" said Joey.

The group just nodded their heads in response. In the distance, there was a cracking of a branch. The sound of someone walking in the wilderness, the darkness. They all grab their flashlights and shine them in the direction of the sound. Nothing, absolutely nothing there. Not an animal, not a single thing that would show any type of disturbance. Hearts started to beat just a little bit faster. Breathing just a tad bit off kilter.

Brian softly says, "So I did some research on this place. Supposedly there has been a lot of gang murders here. There was also a nun who had some disturbing things done to her and then she was hung."

Katrina angrily, yet still quietly says, "What the fuck. Joey did you know this? Brian, why wouldn't you say something before we left to come here? Is this even safe to be here at all? What if there are gang members here right now?"

"No, I didn't know about that. Brian, why the fuck would you not tell us earlier?" said Joey.

Brian responds with a grin on his face, "Well, we already planned it and were ready to go. I didn't want to have any change in our plans. Besides, it had also said the gangs never come here anymore. The cops started watching for them and would bust them, so no need to fret. Should make for a really haunted place it seems."

Joey smacks Brian on the back of the head. "You idiot. If you get us killed, I am going to kill you again. In a worse way though."

Brian shrugged, "How was I supposed to know you would all bitch out if there was something as simple as gang murders that happened here?"

Dustin growled, "You cocksucker, fucker, god damn lint licker."

Everyone stopped and looked at each other and started laughing.

"Alright, well, we are already here so let's just go make the most of it," said Joey.

They all quieted down again. There was another noise in the darkness. Then another; this time much closer and shorter in time apart. The temperature seems to be dropping again. Realizing that they had not moved very far into this trail, they decided to continue on. Even though they continued to hear movement, it seemed to stay behind in the area by the stairs just ahead on the left hand side. As they walked away, the sounds began to fade away.

As they walk down the trail, they have their flashlights on, but only dim. They don't want to have a bright light on, but they also don't want to step on any animals, like snakes, that could harm them. Trekking ahead, everyone started to get a feeling that they were being watched. Individually, they all felt this. However, no one wanted to mention it to each other. They knew if they freaked out, they all would. It got to the point where the feeling was overwhelming, there was an extreme anxiety that had overcome them all. They stopped in their tracks and grouped together in a circle.

"Ok, I didn't say anything, but I've had a feeling as if we were being watched for a while now." said Katrina.

Joey, Dustin, and Brian and reply, "Me too."

Right when they finished saying that there was a rustling just ahead. They looked and pointed their flashlights, as well as making sure the camera was facing that way. This time, they saw something dart across the trail going behind trees. Again, it goes back from left to right, and right to left. It is moving fast; they can't even comprehend if what they are seeing is real.

"What the fuck was that?" Katrina said softly.

"Uh...uh...I don't know. Maybe it was a coyote?" Brian's voice quivered.

"There is no way that was a coyote. It was bigger, and standing on two legs," said Joey.

"It's probably another person out here trying to see something and is playing a prank on us.

Let's just wait and see what happens," replied Dustin.

They all stood and patiently waited to see what would happen next. Nervous, you could see the illumination shaking from their flashlights shining in the direction of the being they had seen. Not a single one of them could keep it remotely steady, but no one dared to mention it.

Five minutes had passed and nothing had emerged again. Dustin said, "See, it had to of been just another person just messing with us. You all ready to keep going on? We have some more to go up this trail."

Continuing on with the utmost caution now, they slowly make their way up the trail. There is repeated rustling in the bushes and behind trees on both sides of them. Every now and then, one of the group would yell out a "Ha ha, not funny assholes." Or something of that nature. They felt that it must be a person out there trying to scare them away, but The Spirit Brigade doesn't scare away too easily. They had arrived at the first fork in the trail. They were told to follow the left side of the split, opposite of the Sam Merrill Trail.

The noises have increased around them faster. They were committed at this point to seeing it through. However, they were all scared shitless. It could not be a person with the speed of the movement being made. At last, they have reached the second split, which when you take the right side, leading to the steps that was the base of the old mansion. It is of course just the foundation now, but nevertheless, this is the place they have been looking for. They all gradually and slowly walk up the stairs. Breathing in the cold air, realizing that it feels as if it was freezing, their breath is clearly visible as if they were in a winter wonderland. Turning around and taking in the scenery, if it wasn't so scary it might be beautiful with the view of Los Angeles in the distance.

Exploring around a bit, they come across some trees, with painted eyes on them.

"Yea, that's not creepy," said Joey.

"That's fucking weird," added Brian.

"Ok, well I guess it's time to start asking questions? Let's see if we can communicate with Mr. Cobb," said Joey "Hello, is there any entity with us? Are there any spirits within our vicinity that would like to communicate? Is there anything we can do to help you cross over?"

They all waited, seeing if there would be a response. Slowly turning in different directions, that way there are camera views of every angle they could possibly get. The rustling that had been following them the whole time came to a sudden stop. Everything went silent. Not even any of the noisy critters in the wilderness were making a sound. The rustling started up again. However, it was faster, louder. It was more of a trampling, stomping hard and fast. It would start in one spot, stop and appear across to the other side, and repeatedly move around in what seemed like it was the speed of light. It was also as if it was making a pattern of a star. There were no answers, just the fast movement. The movements started to get louder, as if it were branches cracking and breaking off the trees. Large branches came crashing off the tops of the trees surrounding them.

Then, the screams started. Screaming in every which way of where the branches were cracking. It wasn't a normal scream; it was as if one person was screaming in different octaves at the same time. It was so loud, the four of them were petrified, frozen with fear. The screams now started to deepen, a lower tone with every round of screams. Only now, there seems to be words being spoken. These words are not in English, it sounds like a language they have never heard before. The noises and the screams stop again. This has broken the fear trance in Joey.

Joey yells, "This is our chance, fucking run to the car. Don't stop, don't look back."

No one says anything, Joey starts to run while grabbing Katrina's hand to ensure she follows. Immediately, Dustin and Brian follow in a full-on sprint. They jump down the stairs and continue on. They get to the fork in the road and follow the correct path to the car. As they are running down the dirt road that leads them back to the street, Katrina falls to the ground and screams.

Katrina yells, "Something grabbed my ankle and tripped me."

Dustin helps her up being he was following behind her. Her face is pale white, she is freaking out. Joey grabs her hand, and they continue back down the road. Right when they get to the gate to go around and go to the street, they stop and turn around to get one last look. They see a silhouette of something around the area where Katrina said her ankle was grabbed. They could not tell what it was, and they didn't want to stick around to see what it was either. They ran out the gate and got into Brian's car.

Brian drove away as fast as he could without crashing his car. No one said a word for the first ten minutes of the car ride home. Katrina lifted her pant leg to look at her ankle. There were distinct red marks that appeared to be in the shape of a hand.

"What the fuck was all that? My ankle has actual red marks that look like a hand grabbed me," said Katrina.

"Holy shit. God dammit Brian. There is obviously some real demonic shit happening here. I think it is safe to say we should not come back here again. FUCK. That was insane. What could that have been? What was surrounding us? I have so many questions. Are you ok Katrina?" said Joey.

"Yes, I think I am ok physically, not psychologically," replied Katrina.

Dustin chimes in, "Holy mother of all fucks."

"Wow. Just wow," said Brian.

These were the only words said for the rest of the car ride home. Once they arrived at Joey and Katrina's home, they all got out of the car. Silently, they all just walked into the garage and sat in their seats of choice.

Joey says, "We need to check out some of this footage."

Chapter 6

No one has moved yet. They are all just sitting and staring into nothingness. It was late, around 2:00AM. They are not even sure how long they have been sitting here in silence. Joey shakes his head and looks around at everyone. Realizing that everyone was still in their trance, it was his duty to break them out of it and talk about the night. It might not be the right time to review the footage.

Joey stands up and walks to the refrigerator where he grabs beers for everyone. He walks to Brian and Dustin and hands them one. He then walks back over to Katrina and gives her one, followed by a kiss on the forehead.

Joey says, "Damn guys, what in the actual fuck did we just witness?"

Dustin says, "What was in those trees? How was it breaking the branches and how was it talking like that?"

Katrina chimes in, "What was that thing that grabbed my ankle? You guys saw it before we took off right?"

Brian nodded his head, "Yea, that was fucking crazy. I can't believe all that shit we saw. I wonder how much of it is on the film. What do you guys think, should we review some of it tonight? I am totally down for that. I don't think I could go to sleep anytime soon any way."

Joey responds, "Originally, I didn't think anyone would be up for it. I figured everyone was too shaken up, or it was too late. But fuck it, I am down too if Dustin and Katrina are."

Joey and Brian look back and forth at Dustin and Katrina.

Dustin smiles, "You know I am in mother fuckers."

Katrina shrugs, "Fuck it, I guess let's keep the beers coming. If I am going to relive this night already, it better be on a different level of consciousness."

Joey got back up and went over to the TV, turned it on and grabbed the first camera, then hooked it up to the computer to download the video file. After the file was extracted to the computer, he opened the file, and the media player opened up. This one appeared to be Brian's camera.

"Alright, looks like you are up first Brian," said Joey.

"Sounds good. I think I picked up a lot of that shit that was happening," replied Brian.

It all starts with them walking towards the entrance. As they went past the gate and start their way up the dirt road, there was an obvious point of view.

"Damn Brian, you really got a good angle on my ass so far. Fucking pervert," teased Katrina.

"I didn't do it on purpose. I was just walking behind and the way the camera sits on the front of me. I am sure it would've picked that up no matter who is in front of me," replied Brian defensively.

"Calm down, I was just messing with you." As they watched the video, there was something evident that neither of them had seen in the background. There were silhouettes of a person, or possibly people in the woods in the distance. They were continuously moving, more like gliding from side to side. The odd thing about them was that it would look like one in particular would go across but immediately go across again from the original side. Katrina was the first to notice the beings, "Um, guys. Do you see that in the trees towards the back, there are fucking people...well what looks like people just moving around, how the fuck did we not see them?"

As the guys watched what Katrina pointed out, they all just sat in silence. Chills ran down their spines as they realized they were not alone the entire time on their excursion. They continued to watch, the more they saw the more they were getting scared. These beings were constantly poking up near them, sometimes almost standing next to them. However, there was never a clear shot of their faces. It was always a blur. Almost as if they were wearing a mask, but a blank one. No eyes, just black holes where they would be. No nose, just a black hole shaped like a nose. No mouth, not even a line appeared to be where the mouth would be.

"This shit is fucking scary. We should watch Katrina's camera next. They got close to her and grabbed her ankle. I wonder if there could be a better image of them," said Joey.

Katrina shuddered with the thought of them grabbing her ankle and being that close to her without her even knowing.

After they started watching the video and repeatedly seeing the same being again, it almost appeared that it was following Katrina closer than the others. When it came to the point where they were standing and hearing all the screams with the entity zooming around in the star pattern, they realized it was just the one being. The one that looked like it was wearing a mask. How was it making all those screams? How was it moving so fast, and what appeared to be not even moving any of its limbs while doing so? How was it around them the whole time without them seeing it, unless it could only be seen when it wanted to be seen...

Finally arriving at the part of the video where Katrina was tripped, she had turned around when she hit the ground. Clearly you can see a long arm that had come out from the darkness of the trees. An arm that was longer than humanly possible. The scariest part of it all is that no one saw the arm when this had happened.

"I think it's safe to say let's not go to any places where there were violent murders committed.

Especially ones of recent, or ones that have a sadistic past," said Katrina.

The boys all nodded.

They all sat in silence again. This time, shock, awe, and many other emotions were taking over. They knew what they had just witnessed was wild, but they didn't realize how crazy of an event they actually had. They could have easily been killed by whatever that thing was. The amount of things that could have happened is leaving them all quiet and questioning their new hobby.

"Wow. Just wow. That shit was insane. What was that thing? What the fuck did we just witness? What did we just get involved in? Are we still in danger? I don't think any of us expected any of that when we started this. Let's be real, I think we all expected it to be like the hotel every time. We stumbled on to something real here. Holy mother of all fucks," said Joey.

"I am really baffled. Like I told you guys when we got there, I knew there had been murders. But I thought it was gang murders. I was not expecting to see whatever that was. Do we continue? Do we go to new places? I know you guys wanted to go to Pioneer Cemetery next, but is that a good idea?" said Brian.

Joey looks around, "What does everyone think? Do you want to continue to do this? The hotel was fun as fuck. This experience was crazy. We did say we wanted to get into this, to see if we can witness some crazy shit and we just did. I say we continue. I say we do make sure there isn't anything like this that had happened there first though. Like let's not go back there, let's find some other places that might not be so dangerous. What say you all?

Katrina responds, "Ok, if you are down Joey, I will always be down."

Dustin's says, "Fuck it, we have come this far. Why not keep going. Besides, we already spent the money on these cameras, might as well get the use out of them."

Brian just nodded his head in agreement. Everyone was still in shock from what they had witnessed that night. After agreeing to continue their new hobby, they sat in silence. They sat without saying a word for about a half an hour until they all passed out sitting.

******

One by one they started to wake up. Groggy, hung over, and confused, Brian was the last to wake. He looked around at everyone still sitting in the same spots, "You guys, was that shit real last night? Did that really happen, or was I just dreaming?"

Joey responds, "Yeah man, that was fucking real. That shit was insane. I hope the cemetery isn't that fucking crazy. I don't think we can all handle anything that crazy."

Katrina says, "Oh man, I forgot we said we would do the cemetery next. I mean, it's the original cemetery of Glendora. Glendora is boring, I highly doubt it will be anything too crazy like what we just witnessed."

"I've only heard it being a fun place. Nothing too scary, but just good ol' wholesome haunting. Not the evil demon type where they are surrounding us to do who knows what like we just witnessed." Said Dustin.

"Fuck it guys. When do you want to go? When's everyone free? I've got next Friday night and Saturday morning free so that's perfect for me and Katrina." said Joey.

Dustin responds, "Works for me too."

Brian adds, "Me three."

Joey nods, "I guess it's settled. Friday night it is. Let's just hope it's going to be a good and safe one."

Being that it is the morning, well closer to noon, Brian and Dustin take off. Joey and Katrina slowly dragged themselves over to their bed.

Joey said, "Hey, do you think it's a good idea that we continue doing this? Are we asking for trouble?"

Katrina turns her head slowly, "Huh....doesn't matter now. We've already committed to this. So I guess we are going to find out eventually when we go to the cemetery."

"I guess you're right. I have a strange feeling about the cemetery. I am not sure why, but it just feels like there is something weird going on there. Not so much like something scary, but something really weird."

"What do you mean? Like some sort of sex cult? People going there to do weird things?"

"Of course you would think it was a sex cult. No, I don't really know. Just a weird feeling about it, that's all. I am sure it's nothing. Do you want to watch some of that footage again from last night? That was hard to believe. If I wasn't there myself, I would think that shit wasn't even real. I would think whoever filmed it was making a movie or was able to edit it somehow."

"For real. It grabbed my fucking ankle and tripped me. How did whatever that was do that? I thought spirits or whatever couldn't make physical contact."

"So did I. Maybe it wasn't a spirit, maybe it was a demon or something. Whatever it was, I hope we never see it again."

Katrina lifted up her pant leg to reveal a bruise where she was grabbed.

"Look Joey, that shit left a huge bruise on my ankle. It is actually shaped like a hand."

"Whoa! That is a hand all right. That bruised fast, too. I am going to take a picture of that right now for evidence. Now if you could kindly remove your pants so I can get a better picture."

"Really Joey, right now? I don't need to take off my pants to take a picture of my ankle. However, I will take them off anyway because I want to go back to sleep. So don't get any funny ideas. I am actually going to sleep."

"Ok, ok. First though, seriously let me take a picture of your bruise. That shit is crazy."

Joey took a few photos of Katrina's ankle and then they both proceeded to go back to sleep.

Chapter 7

Friday night comes around and everyone is excited to get started on a new adventure. This time it is going to be somewhere that they've heard of being haunted their whole lives. This time it is within their hometown. This time feels different. Even though they are still very new to this, something feels different. Not the same as Pasadena. Not the same as the Aztec Hotel.

Of course, it is now around 1:00 AM, when they decided it is time to start heading to their destination. The directions that they received from a friend weren't exactly clear. First, they must drive west on Bennett Avenue until it ends at Barranca. Turn left and go past the train tracks. Then make a right into the first street, which is a little community. Make an immediate right and take that all the way to the end where they will park in the guest parking spots.

The group followed the driving directions, and now they are standing outside of the car looking around, making sure they were quiet enough and didn't wake anybody. This is where the directions get a little confusing.

"Ok guys, we have to hop this wall and follow the train tracks for a little bit," said Joey. "Dustin and Brian, you go first. I'll give Katrina a boost up and you guys help her down the other side."

Everyone nodded and Dustin and Brian hopped the wall. Joey put his hands in front of him interlocking his fingers and bending his knees slightly to let Katrina step into his hands for a boost up. She grabs onto his shoulders and steps in, while he easily lifts her up and she grabbed onto the wall pulling herself up, one leg on and then the other. She was sitting on top of the wall and then dropped forward where Dustin helped her down. Joey took one last look around to make sure they didn't disturb anyone, or that no one was looking at them to possibly call the cops. Satisfied everything is still completely still, he grabs the top of the wall where he pulls himself up and hops over to the other side.

This is where things are going to get a little tricky. They have to follow the tracks down until they see the white tent-like coverings with rows of different plants. It is a nursery, so there are many rows of plants. Another catch, there is security that drives around inside the nursery. So, they will have to be covert to not be caught by them – who will most definitely call the cops for trespassing. The four of them are following the instructions and being on edge to make sure they don't get busted. As they are creeping by the plants, there is a noise coming from the distance. Lights start to show from the darkness.

"Shit, security is coming. Everyone find a place to hide," Joey urgently whispered.

Joey grabbed Katrina and they both laid down underneath a makeshift table that is actually a thick piece of wood laying across two blue barrels that is housing many small house plants on top of it. Dustin ran out of the tent area to get out of the lighting and hid behind a bush. Brian jumped off to the side and covered himself up within the ivy on the ground. The white truck came up to the tented area and slowed down. Taking their time to make sure they take in the environment for any type of disturbance. They were lucky that the security either were tired, not paying attention, or just didn't really care. They should have been seen, but for whatever reason, luck was on their side, and they were not made.

They waited in the silence for a while, for what felt like an hour. In reality, it was only around fifteen minutes, but that silence and cold made it feel like an eternity. They all popped their heads to view and agreed with a nod and moved simultaneously. Continuing on their track of what they think of being the right direction, they get to the end of the canopies. The nursery ends and it leads to what appears to be a hill, but more of a makeshift dirt road. The other side of the road looks to be a drop down into some sort of digging area where it is probably twenty feet down or so, more with a large area of land that has been flattened out and still has construction equipment present.

"This must be the way," said Joey. He pointed up the unpaved road and started to trek his way up. The rest of the group followed him as he directed them to what appears to be a gate. They walk up towards the gate and find that there is a large rock behind the gate, this rock has an engraving in it that says "IN MEMORY OF THE VALLEY PIONEERS. FAIRMOUNT CEMETARY 1876."

"I wonder if they knew they spelled cemetery wrong on the marking," said Katrina.

"I would assume not if it's engraved and not fixed since 1876," replied Brian.

"True," said Katrina.

They all are feeling excited, knowing that they have finally made it to their destination. After sitting there for a few seconds, they realized that they were standing in front of the gate and were in plain sight. If the security was anywhere nearby, they would be seen, and this small accomplishment would've been for nothing.

Next to the gate there is a chain link fence that wraps around the entire cemetery. However, there is a gap in between the gate's cement pillars and the fence. This is where The Spirit Brigade was able to enter their destination. Slowly walking in, they look around. They walk just past where the large tree in the fronts branches are hanging down. This is the spot that gives a clear view of what they will be walking around in.

"This is magnificent!" Dustin emphasized.

Taking it all in, panning their vision from side to side. The right has a group of crosses to what appears to be unmarked graves. Directly ahead, there are graves that have large headstones, large plots that are surrounded by concrete. There are also regular headstones and plots, there doesn't seem to be a rhyme or reason for how the cemetery was planned. There is a flagpole in the middle of the cemetery. This was no ordinary cemetery, besides being from the late 1800s. It was on a hill in its entirety. There were only parts that were created to be flat for the sole purpose of burials.

"I guess we should start the explorations. Do you guys want to split up? Katrina and I can go to the left and you guys can go to the right," said Joey.

"Oh man. This is exactly how every horror movie starts before everyone gets killed. I don't know if that's a good idea after that crazy shit happened in the forest," Brian said.

"Ok. Let's just all stick together then. That's fine, we can hold your hand you little baby. Ha ha ha ha," mocked Katrina.

"You wouldn't be laughing if some crazy shit happened again. What if we were separated from each other and the others were ambushed, how would you feel if we got killed? Or what if they ambushed you and we weren't there to help? Huh, what then?" Brian said.

"Ok, ok, I get it. Don't get your panties in a bunch. I know, I know. You are right, we should all stick together," Katrina replied sarcastically.

They all started to walk right up the middle. It was incredibly quiet. Almost too quiet. There were no noises of any kind. Similar to how it was silent in the forest the other night. This brought uneasiness to the group. Remnant feelings from their previous excursion, they slowed down their pace. Everyone is silent, knowing there was an issue previously when this exact scenario played out. Joey decided it was time for him to break the silence and hopefully bring some of the tension down.

"Hey guys, this place is pretty cool. It almost feels peaceful with how quiet it is. Let's just sit here in the middle for a little while and enjoy what we have found. If nothing crazy happens, I think we could make this a regular hangout spot. What do you think?" said Joey, while a spot to sit down.

Looking around at each other they nodded and agreed. Sitting in a circle, listening carefully for any sort of sound, and any type of disturbance in the distance, yet absolutely nothing happened. This lasted for at least fifteen minutes. Then there was rustling in the bushes by the fence that was nearby; however, while they waited in anticipation, watching where the noise came from, out came an opossum. The tension had risen and disappeared within a short period of time.

"Alright everyone, I think it's safe to call it quits for the night. I also think it's safe to say we need to come back here again. Next time, let's forget the gear, or at least some of it. Maybe bring a few things, but we don't need the body cams or whatever else you guys think. Let's just come back and bring some booze and have a good time. Celebrate a badass hidden gem that is right up our alley – quite literally and figuratively," said Joey.

"Oh fuck to the yeah. Let's get back here and get drunk asap," replied Dustin.

Excited about their new find, the group got up and left in what seemed to be twice as fast as it took them to get there. On their way out they did not see the security patrolling at all. When they were leaving, Katrina had an odd sensation. A feeling of being watched. She looked around, trying to see in the distance the best she could. There was no one in sight, so she just brushed it off and thought she was maybe being paranoid or feeling extra sensitive to the environment.

Chapter 8

It is now next weekend and the friends could not wait to get back to their new spooky, yet safe, hangout spot. They all gathered at Joey and Katrina's per the usual ritual of getting set up and ready to go. This time, they were undecided if they should even bring any type of recording equipment.

Brian questioned, "What's the point of carrying around any of the equipment? It is annoying, gets in the way, and just creates extra steps that we need to do. Why not just hang out there and enjoy the place?"

"I get what you're saying, let's just bring like one camera. I will carry it, but we can just have the one for that just in case scenario," said Joey.

"Besides, we kind of spent some good money on this stuff. We should at least bring one so we don't waste our money," said Dustin.

"Are we calling it quits on trying to find other places or what? I am pretty sure there are other haunted places we can see, too. If we go to other places, that's when we can really gear up," Katrina chimed in.

"Exactly. See, Katrina knows what's up. Not only are you sexy, but you are smart too. Come here and give me a kiss," Joey said excitedly.

It is now 12:00 AM. The Spirit Brigade has gathered all the things they wanted to bring. A bottle of tequila, check. A bottle of whiskey, check. A backpack full of miscellaneous beers, check. A cigarette case with joints, check. Now to the part that usually is the hardest to get ready for the night. Who is going to be the driver?

"I drove last time, so definitely not me," said Joey.

"I'll drive this time and just get my turn over with," said Brian. Then smiled widely. "Besides, we are bringing the tequila."

"Shut up Brian. Joey you should be mad people say things like that about me," Katrina snapped.

"I know I should, but let's be real, you look amazing without your clothes on. At the end of the night, it's always me you come home with anyway. I don't have anything to worry about. Besides, look at that ugly fucker anyway. I almost pity the guy, so I can't be too mad." Joey chuckled.

"Wow, you're a real dickhead," Brian said while laughing.

Katrina busted up laughing, "Ok, I guess you're right. The poor guy can't get a date if his life depended on it."

"Enough about me. Let's just get to the damn car and leave," Brian said while rushing out the door.

Katrina, Joey, and Dustin erupted into laughter. The three of them shortly made their way out to Brian's car. They all pile in while still laughing softly. They then start the excursion to head back to the cemetery. The directions were easy to remember. The four of them have grown up in the small town, so it doesn't take too much to know the different routes they can take to get to wherever they are going. They get to the same parking spot as the previous week. Quietly all hop the wall, handing over their backpacks full of goodies. Last one over is Joey after helping Katrina up the wall.

They all creep their way down the train tracks again, making their way to the nursery where they will have to be on the watch out for any of the security trucks. This time seemed a little different. The nursery wasn't as lit up as it was the time before. This time, it was almost pitch black, besides some of the lights that are solar lights stuck in the ground. These don't provide very much lighting at all. They make it all the way through the nursery and up the hill to get to the gate of the cemetery without seeing the security.

There was an eerie feeling in the air this time around. No one said anything, so they all just went through the gate and proceeded to go to the center where they sat the time before.

"Well, I guess this as good a place as any here to start cracking open our drinks and get our mini party started," said Joey.

Joey walked over to a headstone ten feet away and set up the camera facing where they were going to be hanging out and started the recording. He then walked back to the group and pulled four shot glasses out of his backpack and set them on a flat headstone that was in front of them. Joey took out the tequila and opened the bottle, pouring the shots and winked at Katrina. Brian grabbed four beers out of his bag and passed them out.

"Katrina, a Heineken for you, Dustin, a Negro Modelo for you, here's an Arrogant Bastard for me, and last but still least, a Pabst Blue Ribbon for you, asshole Joey," smirked Brian.

"I see how it is Brian, salty bastard," said Joey. "It's ok, you still won't be getting laid any time soon anyway. Ha ha ha ha."

Katrina and Dustin laughed as well. Knowing the tension was starting to rise between Joey and Brian, Katrina poured another round of shots. Then another. Brian stopped taking shots and was only sipping on his beer for he would be the one to drive home and needed to be sober enough in case of getting pulled over. Joey, Dustin, and Katrina on the other hand had no problem drinking a lot. The four of them started to tell funny stories to each other and couldn't help but get louder and louder as they were getting more and more wasted.

"You guys need to keep it down. You are going to draw some attention to us if you keep being so loud," Brian said frustratedly.

The three drunkards attempted to quiet down, which only lasted for a few minutes. At this point, they were quite a few shots of tequila in, Katrina started to do what she did when the tequila hits. Her top came off over her head. Then dropped her pants. She is now standing in a bra, thong, and shoes, when she skipped off to a large headstone that covered her all the way up to her shoulders where she took off her bra and threw it towards the group. She then took off her panties and threw them as well.

Katrina said, "I need another shot."

Brian said, "I'll bring it don't worry."

"Nice try dickface," growled Joey.

Joey jumped up, grabbed the camera, then ran over and poured a shot. He then continued to follow over to where Katrina was behind the headstone. He stood where Brian could see him and handed Katrina the shot and put the camera on her.

"This one is going into the private collection of course. You guys can't review this night anymore. Ha ha ha," said Joey.

"You know what's one thing I've never done Joey?" whispered Katrina.

"What's that?" replied Joey.

"Streaked through a cemetery," Katrina excitedly whispered.

Just like that Katrina took off running, wearing nothing but her tennis shoes. Laughing, she ran by Brian and Dustin, grabbing the just then poured shot as she passed them. She ran fast, and what seemed like only ten seconds, she had made her way around a big circle and is back to where she started. She then grabbed her pants and put them back on. Not caring about wearing a shirt, she grabbed another beer, walked back and threw on her shirt. She then grabbed her bra and thong and stuffed them into Joey's backpack.

All of the boys were standing there in awe, not believing what they just saw. Joey was still holding the camera and pointing it at everyone.

"Ok boys you can pick your jaws up off of the ground. It's not like you haven't seen a naked girl before," Katrina said.

"This night has gotten so much better than I expected," said Brian.

"Wow. I am a lucky man," said Joey.

Dustin just smiled and blushed. While everyone was in shock, there was something that went unnoticed. A girl walked into the cemetery and started to walk up from the gate. She stopped right next to Dustin, looked at everyone and said, "Hi. What you guys doing here?"

"Holy shit! Who are you? Where did you come from?" screamed Dustin.

"My name is Marija. It is spelled M A R I J A but pronounced like Maria," responded Marija.

"I didn't ask you how you spelled your name. You didn't answer me where you came from though," said Dustin.

"I was just wandering around by the train tracks and heard you guys. It sounded like you were having fun so I thought I would check it out," said Marija.

"Have you ever been up here before?" asked Katrina.

"Yea, a few times. I live really close to here so I tend to walk around here. I like to walk at night, it's peaceful and quiet," said Marija. "Well, I am going to go home now. I don't want my parents to look in my room and wonder where I am. Bye."

The group waved to Marija as she left. They watched as she walked to the gate, went around it and disappeared into the darkness.

"What the fuck just happened?" questioned Dustin.

"She came out of nowhere. She was weird too, like didn't seem normal at all," said Brian. "Well, that definitely killed the moment, just when everything was so good, it had to take a huge u turn."

"Yea, something about her creeped me out, let's just call it a night. What do you guys say?" said Joey.

They all nodded in agreement. Just like that, their fun night was ending. They packed up their things and left the cemetery. They couldn't help but feel a little weird leaving. Something felt a little different. They all felt like Katrina did the first time. No one would admit it, but they all felt as if there were eyes on them as they left, back to the car.

Once they all sat in the car, Joey said, "I know that was kind of a buzzkill and a weird way to end the night. But I say we come back again next weekend. What do you guys say?"

Even though everyone felt weird about it, they all agreed that they should. It was such a fun hangout spot that they didn't want the fun to be ruined by a weird random girl.

Chapter 9

Once again, the crew is gathering at the garage to get ready for what they plan to be another epic party night at the cemetery. Slowly but surely becoming their new favorite place to hang out at. Even though the last time they were there, it did end on a weird note. Little did they know how significant that run in was going to be impacting their futures.

Going down the line of who they wanted to be the driver for the night, it was clear it was going to be Dustin's turn to drive. They always gave Katrina a pass, trying to be a gentleman, Joey just made sure the others didn't try to make her drive because he didn't ever want her to have a chance of getting in trouble while driving. This time around, they decided to have a few drinks before leaving. Just a couple of beers, nothing too much, in case they did get pulled over on the way. Pre-gaming as they would call it. Now, being around midnight, it is time to start their adventure.

"I hope we don't run into that weirdo again," said Dustin.

"Yea me too, that was definitely a buzzkill," agreed Katrina.

"There was something definitely off about her, too. Something didn't seem quite right," added Joey.

"Didn't she seem like the cemetery didn't even phase her? Like we were there to party and get spooked. She was there for shits and giggles," said Brian.

They all stood in contemplation of what each other had gathered about their odd experience. After about thirty seconds, they shook it off and grabbed their bags and headed out to Dustin's car. Per the usual seating situation, Brian sat shotgun because Joey and Katrina were inseparable, even when sitting in a car.

"I am kind of hungry guys; do you care if I stop by and get a few burritos from Del Taco on the way?" asked Dustin.

"You're the driver, you do as you please," said Joey.

So, they took a pit stop at the Del Taco on the corner of Grand and Foothill, which is open 24 hours. Everyone decided they wouldn't mind a little midnight snack, so they parked in the parking lot and ate before continuing their journey.

"That hit the spot. Besides, this cherry coke will make a good mixer for the whiskey," said Joey.

"You fuck ass. I wish I could do the same, but I have to drive," Dustin said pettily.

"I mean, you could definitely have a little bit at least," laughed Joey.

"Yea, I guess you're right. I guess I can have a little bit. But I don't have a drink, which brings me to the next complication. So, I guess we will have to go to the AMPM and see Boss while we are at it," said Dustin.

"Oh shit, Boss. Doesn't he remind you of an old-time mob guy who is probably under witness protection?" said Brian.

"He most definitely does. You should definitely not say that to him though," answered Joey.

Dustin drove over to the AMPM which is just on the corner, right behind the Del Taco. They all went inside even though Dustin was the only one that needed anything to buy. The man they all called Boss, was somewhat of a legend in the small town. Well, at least to Joey and his friends. They liked to make up stories about where he could've come from, and what he might be running from. He was an older gentleman, white hair slicked back. Always wore a short sleeve button up shirt, one that an Italian mobster would wear. He had a gold chain and a gold watch and always wore khaki slacks with shined dress shoes.

He only worked the graveyard shift at the AMPM, and it was easy to tell when he was working. He drove a gold, what appeared to be a 1970 Lincoln Continental. So, there was no confusion if he was in. Whenever you brought your items up to the counter to purchase, he always started off by saying "What's up Boss." Hence the nickname Boss. He didn't take shit from anyone; Joey once witnessed him telling someone to leave or he would bash their head in with a tire iron because they were trying to steal. Although the Spirit Brigade never really made it past more than "hi, or have a good night." They were fascinated by him.

They all went back into the car, now satisfied with all of their beverages. From here, there are only a few blocks before it is time to do the long part of the journey. Same as the last time, they hopped over the wall, and everything seemed darker and eerie. There was no sign of the security once again. It was almost as if they were told not to patrol these parts. They carefully, and still quietly, made their way towards the cemetery. Once they started up the hill that leads to the front gate, there was something different behind the gate. They could see that there was something, or someone, standing in the area that they usually hang out at. The person was wearing all white and what appeared to be a long dress. They were standing with their arms out to their sides and their head tilted up as if they were staring into the sky.

All on high alert, they crept up to the gate being as quiet as possible. As they got closer, they noticed that they recognized the person that was standing there. It was Marija.

"Hey, isn't that the weird girl we saw last time? What is she doing?" said Katrina.

"Fuck, it is. What do we do? Should we just go in there?" said Joey.

"I don't know. I have a funny feeling about this. She really creeped me out last week," answered Dustin.

They sat there and watched, while Marija didn't move an inch. It was as if she was in a trance of some sort.

"What the fuck is that guys? Do you see that?" said Joey, pointing at Marjia.

In shock, everyone just nodded. Not being able to take their eyes away from what they were witnessing. It looked like eternal darkness was closing in around the frozen girl. It was as if shadows grouped together and created a large wave of darkness, engulfing the atmosphere that was the entirety of the cemetery. Then started the chants. It was chants of many people. People that they could not see anywhere.

They started to panic, but didn't want to move so they didn't bring any attention to themselves. Their eyes were also drawn to what they were about to witness. They didn't even know what was going to happen, there was a level of excitement, fear, and uncertainty. The dark wave reached the girl in white. The darkness started to engulf her, but it wasn't normal shadow interaction. It slowly crept up her body, starting from the ground up. Whatever was covered by the dark, was then as if it was nonexistent. Watching this girl disappear in front their eyes was something they couldn't even comprehend. Finally, Marija was gone. It had covered her head, and she had disappeared.

Before they became the next meal for the ever flowing darkness, they decided to book it back to the car. They ran as fast as they could. You would think they were a long distance track and field team with the speed they are running. Not looking back at all, they hurry and get into Dustin's car.

"What the fuck did I just witness? Did that girl just get eaten by shadows?" said Joey, while catching his breath.

"I have no idea. We really need to try to comprehend what the fuck we saw. Should we call the cops?" said Dustin.

"Oh yea, and tell them what? Hey, we were at the cemetery we aren't supposed to be at and we saw a girl get eaten by shadows. I am sure that would fly." said Brian.

"I think we should call anyway. We can call from a payphone. Something that won't let it be known that it was us," said Katrina.

So, she did just that, they went back to the AMPM and went directly to the payphone where they proceeded to call the police station. Rather than tell them the truth, they just said that it looked like they witnessed a girl being taken, a kidnapping.

"Mam, you will have to give a little more information than that."

"I am not leaving my information, just know that there's some weird stuff going on. A girl was taken, it looked like some sort of Satanic ritual. Get cops there fast. I think this girl's life depends on it."

"Hold please."

Katrina did not wait to hear what the response was from the 911 dispatcher. The only thing that she thought was odd, was that before she hung up, she heard the dispatcher talking to someone. Probably her supervisor. Katrina was pretty sure that it was supposed to be on mute, yet it was not. The dispatcher was saying to the other person, "Isn't that the area that is off limits to us? What are we supposed to do? If there is something like that going on, are we really supposed to just ignore it?"

After hanging up the phone, Katrina just hung her head down and paused for a moment. Everyone was staring at her with anticipation, wondering what the cops would say about that wild situation. Eventually, Katrina picked her head back up and looked at everyone slowly. Katrina had tears in her eyes.

"Baby, what's wrong? What did they say?" said Joey.

"They basically said they couldn't do anything. They said they weren't allowed to go there. That girl is fucked," said Katrina.

In shock, the four of them kept looking back and forth at each other. They were in disbelief. After a minute, they all quickly ran back to the car to leave. Not wanting the police to track the call to the pay phone; they wanted to make sure that they stayed off that radar.

"I don't get it. How are the police not allowed to go to a cemetery? I know it's kind of in the middle of nothing. It is by a nursery. How would they not be allowed there? It's a part of the town, isn't it? The town the police is paid to protect?" Joey ranted.

"I know, I know. It doesn't make any sense at all. What the fuck do we do? We can't just leave her there. Or wherever she is now that the darkness took her. But what the fuck was that? I don't want to be disappeared, too," said Katrina.

"Fuck that shit. That place is a bad idea. I don't think we should ever go there again," said Brian.

Not even realizing it, but Dustin had been driving around the city not taking them to any destination. They were on Sierra Madre which was the street directly above the cemetery. They just so happen to be passing by the exact spot above the cemetery.

"You dumb ass. You took us in a big circle and now we are driving past the cemetery. I guess everyone should look to your right. Maybe we can see if something is going on," said Joey.

"Oh shit, balls, fuck. Sorry," said Dustin.

As they looked in the direction of the cemetery, there was nothing that could be seen. The cemetery is too far from the road to be visible. However, there is a private road that leads down near the cemetery. When they went, they did notice that there was a farmhouse probably a few hundred feet away from the cemetery, but they never thought anything of it.

"Do you think that is where you get to that farmhouse?" said Katrina, as she pointed to the almost invisible side road.

As Katrina pointed, two headlights turned on down the private road. They all jumped back in their seats.

"What the fuck. Why would someone be leaving there right now? Do you think they are coming to look for us? Do you think the cops let them know about us? This can't be good," Brian said shakily.

To their dismay, the truck turned right. It is now following 100 feet behind them. The truck started to speed up as if it was trying to catch up to them.

"Fuck. Fuck. Fuck. What do I do? Should I speed up and try to lose them?" said Dustin, worryingly.

"Maybe we should just drive normal and act like we are unaware of them. Pretend like we know nothing is going on. Besides, they are coming fast and I don't think we can outrun them now," said Joey.

Dustin nodded. They all sat stiff as boards. They continued to drive east on Sierra Madre, coming close to Glendora Mountain Road. The truck sped up, and even though it is a one lane road, pulled to the right and sped up to get side-by-side with Dustin's car. Naturally, everyone in the car looked to the right. It was an old Ford truck, probably a 1950s. The driver and passenger didn't look like people, it looked like cloaks. No face, not even hands, just two cloaks driving the truck. The head position of the cloaks was faced towards them.

"Am I tripping or does it look like empty cloaks are driving the truck and looking at us?" Brian, whimpered.

"Holy shit. I don't even see hands on the steering wheel," said Joey.

The driving cloak's arm pointed right to the group.

"Fuck, fuck, fuck. There isn't a hand in that cloak. What the fuck is that shit?" shrieked Katrina.

After the cloak pointed at them for a few seconds, the truck slammed on its brakes. As soon as it was far enough behind their car, it made a sudden u-turn. It was fast. So fast that the truck lifted up on two wheels as it made its turn. It sped off faster than it did to catch up to them.

Dustin made it to Valley Center where he will be turning right to head towards Foothill Avenue.

They were all flabbergasted. Dustin was slowly driving down Valley Center, not going over 20 MPH. They were all in utter shock and disbelief.

"What does that even mean? Why did it just point at us. How did they even do anything at all. There was no one even there. Am I delusional? Maybe I should have paid more attention. Maybe I've lost my mind?" Dustin said while freaking out.

Brian slapped Dustin across the face to snap him out of his panic.

"If this was different circumstances, I would slap a tooth out of your big dumb face. Considering what's going on, I understand. You still have a big dumb face," said Dustin with a straight face. Everyone in the car looked around at each other and started to laugh.

"You have a big dumb face, Brian. Ha ha ha ha ha," Joey erupted.

The laughter continued for a few minutes before the group drove back to Katrina and Joey's garage. Everyone did not want to admit what they just saw. Not wanting to acknowledge the madness they had witnessed. Not wanting to discuss the possibilities that might be heading their way. They each knew that this was a sort of crucible. This was going to change their future. This was going to affect them in more ways than they even knew.

Chapter 10

Dustin and Brian decided to stay the night, didn't want to take the chance of seeing the mystery truck driving cloaks. Although there wasn't much conversation happening, they all could not sleep. They just lay in the dark, well they kept the TV on because no one wanted to admit it, but they didn't want to be in the dark after what they saw. This time, even though they usually only watch horror movies together, they watched a comedy.

"Ok guys, we have to talk about what we saw last night. First let's start with the girl getting abducted by shadows. What. The. Fuck," exclaimed Joey.

"Yea, I don't know. There was something really off about that. The time before, when we first met her, there was something off that day too. She seemed to know something but acted off. Then last night, she didn't seem to care that she was being taken. Or, well, I don't know. Something was just... off," said Katrina.

"What in the fuck did we get ourselves caught up in? Ok, first there was that madness we saw in Pasadena. Like how did we just forget that happened and keep going on? We must be dumb asses. Then we see shadows take a girl and disappear. Oh, to top it all off, we see a cloak driving a truck with no one under it. Then, I assume it was pointing at us. That isn't terrifying at all," ranted Brian.

"I honestly don't even know what to think anymore. That shit was wild. All of it. What do we do now? We have this crazy knowledge of something happening in our hometown. We even tried to tell the police; they said they couldn't do anything. The real question is, do we go again, or do we run away from this and try to forget it even happened?" asked Dustin.

"Ok, you know there is something wrong going on when Dustin is being this serious and not saying something weird," said Joey.

Everyone giggled but stopped after a few seconds and just looked back and forth to each other.

"He's right, what do we do? Maybe we should just wait for a few days. Not jump to conclusions right away. Let's just try to process this madness. In a way, this is what we originally signed up for in the first place. We created The Spirit Brigade for reasons exactly like this. I for one never thought we would see anything this crazy though. We have a lot of things to think about."

They all sat in silence and stillness for the next ten minutes.

BAM BAM BAM,

Loud knocks smashed on the door. No one moves, wide eyed they all slowly look back and forth to each other as if they didn't believe what they just heard. They wait, see if it happens again. No sound.

BAM BAM BAM

It happens again. Once again, no one moves. They all look at Joey, it is his place after all.

"Hey dipshit, it looks like your friend's car got keyed last night. Just wanted to let you know," Frank yelled from behind the door.

"What? Someone's car got keyed? You would want to be the one to deliver the bad news you asshole," yelled Joey.

Frank smacked the door one more time and then walked off. They all looked at each other and jumped up throwing on their shoes and ran to the door to see what vandalism had happened to one of their vehicles. They barrel out the door and run to the street. Joey's car has nothing on it. They run to Brian's, nothing. They run to Dustin's and on the driver's side door, there is a deeply engraved symbol. The symbol is within a circle, which is oddly perfectly formed. The symbol appears to be some sort of weird sigil.

"Fuck me. What does this mean? This has to of been those damn invisible cloak people, right?" said Dustin concerned.

"Shit. Not only do they know your car, I assume they now know where I live," panicked Joey.

"Maybe it's just some type of warning. Like telling us to stay away or something," Brian whimpered.

"Ok guys, I think you should stay the night again tonight. I don't know what this means, but it's probably safer if we stick together," said Katrina.

They all agreed that they should stick together. They should figure out what this means and what exactly could possibly be in store for them. Unfortunately for them, they have no idea what or who could possibly be behind any of it. They were already freaked out by what they had witnessed, now there is an uncertainty that is sitting in the pits of their stomachs. An uneasiness that they just can't shake. The worst part, the day just barely started.

Joey, Brian, and Dustin were all scheduled to work but they decided that it would be best if they called out. There was a worry within the room. A lingering sense of doom. Everyone was hungry, but they had a loss of appetite. The overwhelming anxiety building up in the room. Everyone is silent, staring at the wall. No one is moving, the energy is building with negative thoughts.

"Fuck! We need to snap out of this funk. Let's not jump to crazy ideas or scenarios of what might be in store for us. For all we know, it was a simple warning and as long as we mind our own business, we should be perfectly fine. Right guys?" said Joey.

Everyone shook their heads, looked around and nodded in agreement. Although hesitant and a little cynical reactions in the end, everyone somewhat agreed.

"I bet tonight everything will be fine. We can just hang out here. Watch some movies or something and act like nothing even happened. We can put this behind us and just move along. What do you say?"

"Fuck, I don't know. We can try, but that is going to be incredibly hard to try and forget. Not to mention the thoughts of what might be heading our way. I will stop there. Let's just hope there is nothing to worry about," Brian chimed in.

"I don't know about you guys, but I am getting hungry. We should go get something to eat. What does everyone feel like?" said Dustin.

"I am always hungry. I feel like a nice big breakfast burrito. That sounds amazing to me," added Katrina.

"Yes! Let's go to Grand Burger. I can get some zucchini fries with ranch dressing. Holy mother of fuck yea," Dustin said excitedly.

They all agreed Grand Burger sounded good, so they all slowly dragged themselves out to the street. To decide whose car to take was going to be settled by a few games of rock, paper, scissors. Joey lost two out of three rounds of the rochambeau , so it was decided that his car was the chariot for the excursion. They quickly get into the car and back out of the driveway. Joey slowly drives past Dustin's car and looks at the sigil engraving.

"That shit is crazy; how did they make is so symmetrical?" said Katrina. "I would be impressed if it wasn't so scary at the same time."

"My poor vehicle of transportation. Why must they tattoo you with evil signs?" Dustin whimpered. "Now people around town will see how you have been violated. This means war."

With Dustin mentioning those final words, the rest of the passengers looked around at each other. Their eyes equally have a look of fear for their unknown future. As quickly as their eyes all met, they equally found another focal point.

"Well, I guess you're kind of right Dustin. I think we are going to be stuck in this against them. Whoever they are. We have been marked. Maybe that does mean we will be at war. I hope not. That was scary," Joey calmly stated.

The rest of the drive was in silence. No one turned on the radio, there was no conversation to be had. Just a dreary and quiet expedition to the destination of sustenance. Arriving, it was obvious no one wanted to get out of the car, Joey made his way to the drive through.

"Welcome to Grand Burger, what can I get for you?"

"One moment please," said Joey. "Ok, what does everyone want?"

Oddly enough, everyone decided they wanted to have the same thing. Fried zucchini with ranch to dip it in and a large orange bang.

Satisfied with their order after receiving it at the window Joey drove off to make his way back to his home. All four of them drinking their orange bangs faster than they should, the drinks were definitely not going to make it the whole trip. Joey realized this and set his drink down while grabbing the bag for his zucchini. After a second, Joey decided he was going to save the food for when he got home.

Joey was heading north on Grand and instead of turning right on Bennett to head towards home, he kept going north. Everyone realized that he didn't make the turn, which would mean only one thing. He was heading towards Sierra Madre, where they had their interesting encounter with the bodiless driving cloaks. What took everyone by surprise, Joey turned left, now heading in the direction of the cemetery.

The car stayed silent. This time the energy was full of anticipation, panic, and complete worry. Now they knew they couldn't actually see the cemetery from the street, but they could see down the driveway where the truck had come piling down. They had arrived where the driveway was, Joey slowed down to have a better look. They could see the truck, parked in the spot where they initially encountered it. As they were staring trying to get a better look at what was around the truck, or what the home looked like, flashing red and blue lights appeared in Joey's rear view mirror.

"What the fuck. Why am I getting pulled over?" asked Joey as he pulled his car to the side of the road.

Joey put his car into park, turned off the ignition, and rolled down his window. A Glendora Police officer walked up to his window and stared at him without saying anything for five seconds. The five seconds might be a short time, but to Joey and the crew, it felt like a lifetime.

"Do you know why I pulled you over?" said the officer.

"Um, no actually. I have no idea why you pulled me over," answered Joey.

"What were you doing back there?"

"What do you mean? I was just driving."

"No. I could see that you had slowed down significantly, and it appeared like you were looking down that driveway."

"Oh that? Yea I had never noticed that driveway before. I wanted to see what it was. I wasn't sure if it was to a house or just an empty lot or something. There's no address or anything so I couldn't tell."

"Do yourself a favor son, don't go peaking your head into any business that you might end up regretting in the future."

"What? What do you mean by that?"

"There was a disturbance the other night. In this near vicinity. You wouldn't happen to know anything about that would you, Joey."

"No, I have no idea what you're talking about."

Before Joey could finish his sentence, the officer had turned around and walked back to his car, got in, turned on his sirens and drove off while peeling out next to Joey's car.

"Wait. What the fuck just happened. He knew my name," said Joey.

"Yea, he pulled you over. They check your license and things when they pull you over numb nuts," said Brian.

"He never asked for anything. My registration is still in the glove compartment. My wallet is still in the center console. How the fuck did he know my name? Why did he mention the other night?"

Sitting and contemplating what they had just witnessed, a new feeling of unsettledness overwhelmingly took over the car. Once again, they continued to drive home. Driving in silence, no one knew what to say. No one knew what to do or how to break the ice, cold silence that inhabited the vehicle cab.

"You're right Joey. You didn't show him your license or anything. How the fuck did he know your name. Why was he mentioning the other night? Shit just got a whole lot weirder," said Katrina.

After continuing their drive and now turning down Live Oak Ave to get back to Joey's, Dustin noticed that there was a car following them.

"Um not to be the bearer of bad news, but I am pretty sure that black car behind us has been following us since we got pulled over."

"Ok, let's test this theory out. I am going to make four right turns so we go in a circle," said Joey.

So, Joey took the first right on Northridge Avenue. He then proceeded to take a right on Cullen Avenue. Next, was another right back onto Sierra Madre once again. Finally, the last right turn back onto Live Oak. Joey looks in the rearview mirror. The car is not in sight.

"See, I don't think they were actually following us. Maybe you are just getting extra paranoid Dustin."

The black sedan came skidding down Live Oak off of Sierra Madre. The car is speeding behind them, only now the car is swerving back and forth between both sides of the street.

"Holy shit. What the fuck. They are following us, and now they are flying up behind us driving like a mad man," screamed Dustin.

Not knowing what to do, Joey decided to pull the car over. He stopped the car and waited to see who was driving the vehicle that had been following them. The car swerved all the way to the left of the street, where there is a car parked on that side of the street parallel to where Joey's car was stopped. Looking over, Joey noticed that the black car was now barreling directly towards the parked car. The black car smashed directly into the car, which was a Suburban.

Both cars completely crunched after a loud bang of destruction. Automotive pieces were flying everywhere. Different color of fluids shooting into the air.

"WHAT THE FUCK!" screamed Joey.

They all jumped out of the car to go see if anyone was hurt. They get to the black car, for the Suburban was already parked and did not have anyone inside it. No one was in the black car as well. Empty. No one was in the driver's seat. No one was in the passenger seat. As well as no one was in the back seats. No one. Joey looks around to see if maybe someone was ejected from the impact and was launched from lack of seatbelts, but there was not a single body to be seen.

Just then, someone from the house from where the Suburban was parked came running out.

"Oh my god. What the fuck just happened?" yelled the woman running out of the house. "Is everyone ok? Is there anyone hurt? I'mcalling 911."

"I don't know how to say this lady, but there is no one in the car. We were parked across the street and this car came flying down the street and just slammed into your SUV. I didn't see anyone get out of the car, nor did I see anyone fly out of the car. But there is no one in sight either," exclaimed Joey.

"Wait, what? What do you mean there is no one? There has to be a driver," she said.

"I know. It doesn't make any sense. But I saw the car smash into yours. No one got out of the car, no body ejected anywhere. We sat here the whole time," said Joey.

The two vehicles have now ignited and started to produce a large flame from their conjoined hoods.

"Just to be sure, look inside that car. See if you can open a door or something. You wouldn't just want to let someone die, would you?" she suggested.

Joey and Dustin looked at each other with a worried and concerned look then shrugged and walked towards the car. They went to opposite sides and opened the front and rear doors. No one was there. In fact, it had looked like there hadn't been a body within the car in a long time. There was a layer of dust that had covered the seats, all of them.

"See ma'am, not a single person within this car," said Joey.

The flames grew higher and started to expand, which brought concern to Katrina.

"Hey guys, hurry up and get over here, it looks like it's going to blow," Katrina yelled.

The front driver side tire on the suburban exploded. It was loud and sounded like there was a bomb going off. Dustin and Joey screamed, "Oh fuck," simultaneously and ran towards the sidewalk where everyone was standing. They all agreed they should get even further away from the vehicles and followed the lady back up by her house.

Joey was standing on her lawn and taking deep breaths to try and calm himself down after being so close to the exploding tire. During this time, he started to think and realized something, how did the lady get outside so fast? Why did she not really seem fazed by it? Joey started to think, what if this lady was a part of it all and was just here to act as a decoy? Joey shook his head and laughed to himself. Thinking that it must be a coincidence.

Just then two police cars came flying from around the corner. As well as an ambulance followed behind them. Joey noticed that one of the police officers was the one who had just pulled them over and said those weird things to him.

"Shit, look guys. It's that weirdo officer that had just pulled us over and said all those weird things. Of course it would have to be that guy. Something seems off," said Joey.

The paramedics stepped out of their emergency vehicle and ran up to the cars.

"Is anyone hurt? Is anyone trapped inside of the vehicles?" said the female paramedic.

"Hi ma'am, no one is hurt and no one is inside the cars. You see, it was the weirdest thing. There was no one in the car when it crashed into the other car," said Brian.

"No one was driving? How is that even possible?"

"We were wondering the same thing honestly."

More sirens were coming around the corner. A large red fire engine came barreling down the street and slammed on the brakes while simultaneously honking the horn. The fire fighters jumped out of the truck while hooking up the hose to the nearest fire hydrant that conveniently was right next to the burning cars. The flames were extinguished.

"So, troublemakers, it didn't take long until I see you again. What the fuck did you do to cause this?" said the asshole officer.

"We didn't do anything. We were parked across the street and the car came plowing into the other one. There was no one in the car, it just rolled into the other one. Then kaboom, explosion. Next thing you all are here," said Joey.

"Hmmmm....not sure I believe all that. Let me go ask this nice lady, she will tell me the truth. If you are lying though, best believe I will throw the metaphorical book at you."

They watched as the officer went to speak to the lady. She looked up at them a couple of times while talking, she also pointed at the vehicles as well as Joey's car. The officer started to make his way back to the car.

"Alrighty then, it looks like it's your lucky day. She said it the way you said it. For once in your worthless lives, it looks like you told the truth," the officer immediately turned around and walked away as he was finishing his sentence.

"Ok, I guess that means we are free to go. That's the second time this guy just finished his sentence and walked away without explanation. Let's get the fuck out of here before it gets even crazier," said Joey.

The group all went back to Joeys car and got into their seats and continued down the street to get back where they can try to understand what has been happening around them.

"Is anyone else as scared and confused as I am?" asked Katrina after sitting down inside the room.

"I think it's safe to say that we are all confused and a little bit scared. Ok maybe more than a little," replied Joey.

Once again there is silence. The four of them ate in silence, no TV, no music, no conversing. Just eating in the quiet of the room.

"I know it's the middle of the day, but I say we drink and loosen up a little bit. This is weird and it's making me uncomfortable," said Katrina.

Day drinking was going to commence, it was what followed they weren't prepared for.

Chapter 11

Eating their food that they had picked up from Grand Burger, they decided it was the perfect time to drink beers to wash it down and raise the spirits a bit. Even though after all that time, the food ended up cold, they didn't care and just ate it anyway. After two beers, Katrina decided it was time to add the hard alcohol to the mix.

"Fuck it guys, let's just get drunk. Who cares if it's in the middle of the day. We don't have any type of obligation for the day, no one works, no one has any plans. If you do, cancel them. Let's just try to have a good day and night and forget any of this happened. I am even going to drink the tequila."

"Damn, looks like today is going to get even wilder. Hopefully we can just have a good day, and even better night, then we can try to forget all of what's going on in our town," said Joey.

So it began. One shot of tequila turned into three. One beer turned into four. In a short period of time, the whole crew was feeling quite good. Music was blasting, and everyone was having a good time. Katrina put on "What is love?" by Haddaway.

"Oh shit! Fuck yea here we go," Katrina yelled, as she started to dance after jumping onto the couch.

Dustin, Brian, and Joey were playing darts when Katrina ran over and pulled Joey to her. She started dancing on him, "Ok guys, you can skip me now. I won't be finishing the game," Joey said.

Joey wasn't much of a dancer but definitely enjoyed when Katrina would be dirty dancing all over him. He could follow her lead, but mostly just stood there while moving slightly to not look like he didn't do anything at all. Whenever Katrina would get buzzed, she always had the urge to dance the night away. That was the cue that she was on the brink of getting drunk and needed to start adding in some water, which Joey would always be the caring boyfriend and bring to her.

Now, being that it is still the middle of the day, it was time to start pacing themselves, otherwise they might end up passed out drunk before the sun even went down. That being said, Katrina was drinking tequila, and we all know what happens when she drinks tequila. Katrina was still dancing, she had pushed Joey on to a chair where she proceeded to start giving him a lap dance.

"This is definitely going to make me forget about the wild shit that has been going on," said Joey.

Katrina, sitting on his lap, pulls her top off and swings it over her head. She then gets off of him and turns her back to him where she then removes her pants. Now just in a bra and thong, she sits back on his lap and kisses him.

Not taking his eyes off of Katrina, Joey yells, "Brian, Dustin. We are going to need some alone time for a bit."

"Mother fucker. Every damn time. You sure we can't just stay for the show?" said Brian.

"Nope, time for you to get the fuck out. Ha ha ha," laughed Joey.

As Brian and Dustin started to walk towards the door, Katrina removed her bra. She stood up and turned around, but she was covering her breasts with her hands. She sat back down on Joey where he had replaced her hands with his. Brian and Dustin were slowly walking towards the door, watching, but trying not to make it too obvious. Katrina started to slide her panties off, but kept her legs together to keep her privacy. She looked up at Brian and Dustin at the door, smiled big and waved goodbye to them. Joey waved as well, in which he forgot he was covering Katrina, so one of her breasts was exposed. In which he realized what he did, then took off the other hand and smacked his forehead with both hands. He then started laughing, realizing that he did that. Katrina was not a very shy girl, very confident in her beauty. She stood up and turned around to sit on Joey facing him.

Katrina said, "Close the door on your way out."

Brian and Dustin said at the same time, "Okkkkaaaayyyyyy."

They stepped outside, but after a few seconds Brian peaked his head back inside. Katrina was walking to the door to lock it.

"Close the door you pervert," Katrina yelled while laughing.

Brian closed it quickly. The door lock clicked. Dustin and Brian decided to play a game of horse with the basketball hoop in the backyard to kill some time.

After a few games of horse, they finally heard the door open, and Katrina stuck her head out of the door. "You guys can come back in now."

Brian and Dustin came back in looking at Joey and Katrina sitting on the couch, then started clapping.

Dustin said, "Ok fuckers. Literally. You good now? Got it out of your system?"

Joey said with a smile on his face. "Yes, we are definitely feeling good. Let's keep this party rolling. I don't know if this day could get any better now. I mean, it started off bad but really took a turn for the best."

"Yea, yea, we get it. You don't have to rub it in our faces," said Brian.

"Get yourself an awesome girlfriend. You won't have this problem if you do that. Ha ha ha," said Katrina.

"So....do you guys want to watch a scary movie again? Maybe we should watch some sort of ghost type movie. Who knows, maybe we will learn something that could possibly help us in some sort of way," said Joey.

They all just sat for a few seconds, contemplating whether this was a good idea or not.

"Fuck it. I say we do just that," said Dustin. "Now the hardest question is, what movie shall that be?"

"I know," said Brian. "It's not exactly a ghost movie, but it kind of is. The setting is in the woods, so it kind of fits what we are going through, too. Let's watch The Blair Witch Project."

"Yea that kind of does fit the criteria, I guess. Fuck it, sounds good to me," agreed Joey.

Joey gets up and sets up the movie. He then grabs a beer for everyone to enjoy while watching the movie.

"Wait. Before we start, we should order a pizza or something. I am getting hungry again," said Katrina.

"Yea, pizza does sound good. You guys good with that?" asked Joey.

Dustin and Brian both nodded their heads in agreement. Katrina picked up the phone and called in to order pizzas. She ordered three large pizzas. One with pineapple, pepperoni, olives, and jalapeños, the second all meats, and the third, just pesto sauce and cheese.

"Ok, pizza is ordered. Should we wait for it to get here to start the movie? Or do you want to just start it and pause when it gets here?" asked Katrina.

"Wait a minute. I just thought about something. Let's watch the second Blair Witch Project. It's a way better movie. Not all documentary style and honestly has more context to it. Everyone agree?" said Joey.

Katrina and Brian nodded. Dustin said, "I have never seen that movie. So that sounds good to me. Let's wait till the pizza gets here to start it. I don't want to have any interruptions while watching a movie I have never seen. For now, let's play a quick game of darts and drink some more beers."

Everyone was in agreement, got up out of their seats, grabbed another beer, and made their way to the dart area. They always tried to be somewhat gentleman, well at least when it came to playing games and letting the girls go first. Katrina was up and they had to figure out who would go next. So, they decided to do what they always do to decide these kinds of predicaments. Rock, paper, scissors, of course. Next would be Dustin, then Brian, and last but not least, Joey would go.

Several rounds go by until they are getting close to finding a winner of the game. They are playing 301, and of course Katrina is in the lead with only needing to get 17 points to win. It is now her turn, and right off the bat she gets a ten, then a six, and last throw she gets a one.

"Mother fucker. I always lose at this game. I don't want to play this shit anymore," said Brian.

"What a fucking crybaby. Maybe you should just practice more so you can get better. We all lost too," said Joey.

"It also doesn't help that I am just that good at this game. Maybe next time I will take it easier on you guys....Yea right. Ha ha ha ha, if you want to beat the champ you have to beat the champ," said Katrina.

Knock, knock, knock

"Oh shit, the pizza is here. Let me go get the door," said Joey.

Joey went to the door, grabbed the pizzas and brought them back inside. He then set them down and grabbed a couple of paper plates. He handed one to Brian and then Dustin. Joey grabbed a few slices of the pesto with cheese pizza and handed it to Katrina. Then he grabbed himself a few slices from the pineapple and other toppings pizza. Dustin and Brian get their plates ready and then they all proceed to take their seats to get ready to watch the movie. It is no longer mid-day, but it is starting to get into the evening. The sun is starting to set, so the ambiance of the movie is settling perfectly.

Joey starts the movie and sits down next to Katrina. After around twenty minutes, they are really starting to get into the movie.

"Do you guys think anything like this could be real?" asked Brian.

"I mean, we kind of lived something very similar to it. Don't you think? From watching that girl get devoured by shadows, to the madness in the haunted forest. I would say any of this is possible. Which is scary as shit if you think about it," answered Joey.

Scratching noises came from the garage door. Although the garage door was insulated, somehow there was a scratching noise coming from it. Everyone froze and looked at one another. Gauging each other's reactions, trying to figure out if they are hearing what they appear to be hearing, or if this is a figment of their imagination. Unfortunately, they all noticed that they are all having the same similar reactions. Which could only mean one thing, they are absolutely hearing the noises.

"What the fuck is that?" said Joey. "There should be no way that we even hear something like that with all the insulation."

"Maybe we should go check it out?" said Dustin.

"Yea.... I guess we should. Let's walk around the side though, that way we can have the element of surprise," said Joey.

"Should we think this through better? What if there is something crazy waiting there for us? What if this is some sort of setup? Like a trap," asked Brian.

"It's now or never, and I personally don't want to wait to see what would happen next," said Joey.

The four of them went out through the back and started to go around the side. They walked as quiet as they could, tip toeing, trying to be like stealth ninjas. They paused right before the end of the pathway where they will be confronting whatever it is that could be waiting for them.

Joey looked back at everyone and put up three fingers, using them to count down so everyone is on the same page. One, two, three, and they all run out to see absolutely nothing standing there. They move around the cars in the driveway, trying to see if there are any possible clues of something being in their near vicinity. Nothing.

"Wait, what the fuck is that?" asked Dustin.

"Oh fuck no. That looks like the same symbol that was carved into your car door. Now it is carved into the garage door. How the fuck did something do that? How was it so fast? Makes sense on why it was so loud, but how was it so fast?" said Joey.

They stood there for a couple of minutes. Looking around, trying to see if they could possibly find any type of disturbance that could point them in a direction of who, or what did this. It was obvious at this point now that they are being targeted. They are known by what they are assuming to be the cult, or whatever that is from by the cemetery. They all follow back to the garage, where none of them can sit and are pacing around the room.

"What the fuck do we do? This is insane. Never did I think we would get ourselves into this kind of mess," worried Katrina.

"Fuck. Shit. Fuck. Ass. Fuck. Goats. Bitch," Dustin said.

Like usual, after Dustin says something odd, everyone stops, looks at him, pauses and laughs. You can always count on Dustin for a good laugh, even when there is something wild going on. Sometimes, the only way to feel better about what is going on, is to get a good laugh in.

Just as they thought things couldn't get any worse, they did. Joey turned around while laughing and noticed something out of place. There was a paper sitting on his bed. He had an eerie feeling about it but walked over to it anyway. He picked up the paper and read, "Tonight. Midnight. Drive all the way South on Valley Center. Turn left and follow to the top. Don't even think about not going. There will be consequences."

"Oh, fuck guys. Look at this note left on my bed. Shit. Shit. Shit. We have been summoned.

Something tells me we don't want to find out what will happen if we don't go," said Joey.

Everyone looked at the note in disbelief. Not really sure what to do at this point. They had called the police about the cemetery and how the girl was taken. The police had said they couldn't even go to that property. The police had pulled them over and acted funny to them earlier on and even questioned them about just looking in the direction of the property. So, it is safe to say that the police will be of no help. Even in the state of an emergency, there will be no help from them.

That leaves one more question, who would they call if they needed help with something? They had no idea who they could possibly call. Their parents wouldn't believe them, even if they did, they would be of no help. Even worse, they would be putting their parents in danger if they did try to involve them, so that was a no go. Once again, they are back to square one.

"What do you guys think we are heading into? Seriously? What could possibly be there? Are we being set up? This seems like a trap," said Brian.

"How the fuck did they sneak past us and bring this paper in here? We were all right there.

There is no way they could've gotten past us. Unless they are some sort of ghost things like what we saw before. Either version of that story is fucked," said Joey. "What do you guys want to do to prepare for this tonight? This is insane."

They all stayed quiet for a few minutes. All looking at the ground, trying to make sense of the situation, also trying to not freak the fuck out.

"I think it goes without saying that we need to build up some liquid courage for tonight's event. I really don't want to be sober for this. We also shouldn't overdo it. We definitely want to be coherent for whatever the fuck we are running into," said Joey.

Everyone agreed with him. Brian made his way over to the refrigerator and grabbed some beers to hand out. Everything else at that moment seemed irrelevant.

"What could this be, seriously? I don't like this at all. This doesn't seem safe. I didn't sign up for this. I don't know what to do about all this. I don't know if I want to go after all. I mean, what if we are walking into our deaths," panicked Brian.

Dustin slapped Brian across the face. Not too hard, but hard enough to snap him out of it.

"Get yourself together man. We are all in this together. I don't think any of us signed up for this madness. The fact of the matter is that we are here now though. So tough shit. Stop being a crybaby, pull your big boy panties up. Punch yourself in the dick if you have to," emphasized Dustin.

Brian looked at Dustin, "Thanks man. I guess I needed that. I am not punching myself in the dick though."

For the rest of the time, they sat and sipped on some beer. Hoping that it would relieve them of their high anxiety, only it was having the opposite effect. They seemed to grow more and more worried about the outcome they will soon be facing. The later it got, the quieter they all were. The energy in the room started to grow more intense. The anticipation made the time seem to slow down, even though it may seem as if time was flying while drinking.

"Ok guys. It would appear to be about that time that we should probably head out. Time to get rolling on down to the promise land of whatever it is we are walking...or driving into," slurred Joey.

It was decided that Brian was going to be the one to drive them tonight. Joey had just driven them around earlier that day, and Dustin's car had been marked. Naturally that disqualifies him from being the chauffeur for the night. They all stood up, took a last drink and slowly made their way out of the garage and dragged their feet to Brian's car. Time to meet whatever they had in store for them.

Chapter 12

This might be the only time they had ever seen Brian drive following the speed limits, or even going slower. Everyone could feel Brians sense of dismay from the moment they had gotten in the car. No one wanted to speak either, it was a dreadful car ride.

Driving south on Live Oak, making a left turn onto Foothill Boulevard. There are no lights on the street besides the car's headlights. Tonight in particular, was an extra quiet night. When there are usually many cars driving around at this time, there are none. They reach the stop sign and make their turn right onto Lone Hill. Continue down and make another right on Gladstone. Turn left onto Valley Center. Take the road till it ends and go left where the trails are.

Now go all the way to the top. They slowly drove their way up, crossing a bridge and following the winding road. When they get up to what appears to be the top, they stop a little short from getting there.

"Holy fuck balls. Why does it look like there's some sort of security tower?" said Brian.

"Because there is. What the fuck have we gotten into?" said Joey.

They slowly continued up, however there weren't any guards or personnel within the tower. There didn't appear to be anyone anywhere. Confused, they creeped up and pulled to the center of the courtyard. They stepped out of the car, not moving away from their doors and peered around scanning the distance to see if there was any sign of any living thing. Nothing.

"This is weird guys. What should we do?" asked Katrina.

"Well, we made it here, so we complied with what they asked us to do, right? I think we should get the fuck out of here and leave," replied Brian.

"Yup, let's fucking go. This is creepy," said Dustin.

Joey nodded in agreement. They all got back in the car. Brian slowly drove further ahead to where he could make a three point turn to head back out. He started by turning left into what appears to be a parking spot next to a building.

As he pulled in Joey said, "Wait, do you hear that? Roll down the windows."

Brian rolled down all four windows, and it sounded like there were goat noises. The noises were coming from inside the building next to them. Brian started reversing and Joey, being in the backseat looking out his window, looked inside the buildings window.

"Holy shit. There's a video playing in the room. It's playing a video of goats being sacrificed. Not slaughtered, sacrificed. What's worse is the room looks like it's meant for kids to be playing in. What is this place?"

As Brian continued to reverse, he saw the video playing as well. "What. The. Fuck."

Brian started to drive a little faster and had reversed enough that he could make the final left of the turn to start going back down the hill. Not wanting to attract a lot of attention by revving his engine and speeding off, Brian continued at a slower speed, but faster than what he began with. Immediately, as they were heading towards the exit, all the doors of all the buildings opened. They flew open as if the most powerful gust of wind slammed into them, sending them crashing against the walls opposite to them.

People, or what they assumed to be people, stepped out. It was a line of them, just standing in front of the buildings. They didn't move, they just stood and stared. There was something off about these people though, their clothes weren't normal, almost old-fashioned.

"Holy shit. Look, some of them have a chain and some sort of collar on their necks. What the fuck is this? Brian, get us out of here," Katrina said worryingly.

Brian started to drive faster, and all the people lined up outside slowly lifted their arms and pointed at them. There was no other movement from them, just pointing. Right as their car reached the guard tower to start their descent down, something fell onto the hood of the car. They all look and see a goat head staring back at them. Brian slammed on the breaks due to natural reaction, and the head went flying off the hood and rolled down the hill in front of them.

They heard a scream from behind them. That's when they looked back and in the middle of the courtyard was the girl that was abducted from the cemetery. She stood there, looking around. One of the men who had a collar and chain on, was unshackled. There was no one who released it, the shackle just fell off as if there was a remote control to release it. He walked up to her and pulled up a knife where he started stabbing her in the stomach. She screamed again, but she didn't collapse. She continued to stand. The man grabbed some of the blood that was leaking out of her.

He started to walk toward the direction of Brian's car. All the others that were shackled, were released and they all walked towards the girl now. Frozen in fear, The Spirit Brigade was watching in terror. The girl was standing there, and multiple people were repeatedly stabbing her.

"Oh, fuck where did that guy go?" screamed Brian.

The man walking towards them somehow disappeared from their sight, even though he was right in front of them. Then he was next to the driver's side window. He grabbed Brian by the hair, pulled his head back and slapped the blood on his face. He made sure blood went into Brian's mouth as well. He held his hand over

Brian's mouth to ensure he swallowed some. After he was satisfied, he let go of Brian's hair and face and stepped back.

Brian screamed and took off, turning to follow the winding road down the hill.

"What the fuck. I swallowed some of the blood. Why did he do that? How did he just appear like that?"

Everyone was stunned. Speechless.

After a few minutes, Joey said, "What the fuck just happened?"

No one could respond.

No one knew what to do or what to say. Fear was the only option. Brian was driving fast down the winding road that would get them away from this evil place. As they were driving down the hill, they opened their windows because they could hear a faint sound in the distance. It is still the screaming of the girl they had seen. The one that was named Marija. The one that was being stabbed multiple times before they left. The one whose blood Brian had just ingested.

"How is she still screaming? How is she still alive?" said Katrina.

"I really don't fucking know. There is some sort of evil sorcery going on there," answered Joey. "She should be dead. It just doesn't make any sense at all."

They got to the bottom of the hill; Brian didn't hesitate to floor it. He drove as fast as he could to the nearest gas station. Before Brian could even come to a full stop, Joey had jumped out of the car and ran to the payphone.

"Nine one one what's your emergency?" asked the operator.

"In San Dimas, at the top of Valley Center. All the way up the hill. To that weird cult group. Or whatever they are. We witnessed them stabbing a girl. Hurry, get up there. There were tons of them stabbing her. Hurry, get up there. I know she can't be alive though. She was stabbed so many times."

"Hold please."

"Oh, what the fuck. Don't tell me that this is out of their jurisdiction again."

"Hello, I am sorry to inform you that we cannot go to that area. It is out of our..."

Before she could finish what she was saying Joey hung up the phone.

"Fuck. Mother fuck. Fuck. They said the same exact shit. They said they couldn't go up there. How the fuck do these people own the police? I don't like this one bit. What the fuck did we just uncover in our own town."

Confused and scared, they decided that it was a good idea to go back to Joey and Katrina's to at least calm down and try to understand what is going on. The streets were eerily vacant again. It was as if everyone was informed not to be out driving during this time. There was not a single car to be seen. Not even the homeless were in the visible vicinity of driving back.

They arrived at the home with a breeze. Not one stop sign was stopped at. Not one stop light was adhered to. Speed limit? Nope, the only time they were even close to a speed limit was when they had to slow down to make a turn, so they didn't roll the car. Brian didn't even really slow down when it came time to park in the street. Skidding and bouncing off the curb, they made their final destination and even though his car wasn't exactly parked properly, no fucks were given.

"Damn Brian, I am surprised we even made it home safe. But, on another note, maybe you can be a stunt driver when you grow up," Said Dustin.

"FUCK YOU. I HAD BLOOD IN MY MOUTH, AND SWALLOWED IT," Screamed Brian.

"Ok, sorry. I was just trying to lighten the mood. You don't need to get your big girl panties in a bunch."

Brian stopped in his tracks. Looked at the rest of them with complete and utter rage in his eyes. So mad, you can see his eyes start to well up, he flipped them the middle finger, turned around and ran to his car. Without saying anything he jumped into it, started the car and peeled off as if he was driving for Nascar, ready to make a bunch of left-hand turns. For another time of the night, they are left in shock and disbelief of what they are witnessing.

"Well, that happened. Let's just get the fuck inside before some other type of crazy shit happens to us just standing out here," said Joey.

The remaining three followed Katrina in to where they all grabbed a water and sat down.

"Seriously, what the fuck is going on?" asked Katrina.

"It doesn't make any sense at all. How can the police, or sheriffs, not be able to go into certain areas of their towns? How is it that when we say someone is being murdered or abducted, they basically just say, sorry we can't do anything about it. As if they aren't supposed to be the protectors, the law." responded Joey.

"Let's not forget that whatever we witnessed, those weren't exactly people. From what we've seen at the graveyard, or even at the haunted forest, there is some sort of spirit or ghosts doing some wild shit. It was almost as if they were controlled or something," said Dustin.

"Now here is the real kicker. What the fuck was going on with Brian just now? He wasn't acting like himself. Paranoid, yes. But there was some real rage behind him. He did not act like himself at all. Maybe, just maybe, it has something to do with the fact that there was blood put into his system. What if that was meant to happen? What if they planned that? What if that was some sort of ritual?" said Joey.

The three of them sat there. Not saying another word the entire night. They eventually nodded off and fell asleep in their seats.

Chapter 13

Waking only a few hours later, Joey, Katrina, and Dustin opened their eyes. Looking around, trying to figure out if what happened the night before was real or only a dream.

"What happened last night was real, right?" asked Katrina.

"Indubitably real," answered Dustin.

"Fuck. I was really hoping I was just having a nightmare. What do we do now?" said Katrina.

"I have no fucking clue of how we are even to continue our days. Like, how do we just continue on with what we just witnessed? Fuck. I am going to text Brian. Hopefully he made it home, or wherever he was going," said Joey.

Joey proceeded to text Brian.

Hey Brian, are you ok? Did you make it home ok? You took off like a madman last night.

They waited and waited to see if there would be a response. Nothing. No response, not even after thirty minutes.

"That can't be good," Dustin said, breaking the ice of them all just sitting and waiting staring at Joey's phone to see if any vibration would indicate a notification.

The anxiety in the room increased. It was an energy of extreme worry you could feel. There was a loud knock at the door. They all jumped from the tension being broken so abruptly. Joey jumped up and rushed to the door, he opened it. Standing there was not Brian, who they had hoped it would be, but standing there was just Joey's brother, Frank.

"Hey dick weed. You have some fucked up friends. They have a real sick of humor," said Frank.

"What are you talking about Frank?" said Joey.

"Look out front. Last time there were cars being keyed. This time, there are dead crows laid out in the front yard. It looks like there was a massacre of birds," said Frank. "The creepiest part of it, they were formed to be in a pentagram, I think. Or something like it at least."

Frank punched Joey in the arm before he ran off to go back inside. Joey was too freaked out to get mad about being punched and trying to retaliate. Without hesitation, Katrina and Dustin hopped up out of their seats and they all made their way to the front yard. That is when they saw the horrific scene. Sure enough, there was a mass of crows, dead and formed into a pentagram. This didn't make any sense. And how could this have happened in such a short period of time? They didn't even sleep that long.

Standing there, Joey said, "I don't think this is going to be the last we hear from them. In fact, I fear this might only be the beginning."

They were unsure of what to do about the bodies of all the crows. They didn't want to just scoop them up and throw them in the trash. They believed they would at least deserve some sort of burial. Maybe not individual burials, that would take too long. But at least give them a proper burial together. One problem, trying to find something to fit them all in. There was not a box they had that could fit them all. Unfortunately, they had to settle on putting them in a large trash bag. One of the thick black ones meant for yard waste.

Dustin and Joey put on some gloves and put all the crows into a bag. They then proceeded to put them into the trunk of Joey's car. After they were all loaded up, the three of them got into Joey's car and made their way back up to Sierra Madre. This time, instead of turning left like they have been to investigate the cemetery, they turned right. They made their way down to Glendora Mountain Road and turned left. This is where they followed up to where they could make a right onto Big Dalton Canyon Road. They followed this for a while, until they found what they thought would be a suitable spot and not exactly where most people would be hiking at. Joey parked the car, and they all got out. Before he opened the trunk, he took one last look around to make sure no one was near to see them and what they were doing.

Joey opened the trunk and grabbed the bag full of crows. Dustin grabbed the shovels. They hiked up the hill, making sure they were completely out of sight of the street. Also looking around to make sure there are no hikers that could run into them while digging the grave. They are pretty deep within the mountain, so they figured it was probably the best they could do. Dustin and Joey took turns digging. This was going to have to be a somewhat big grave. It is going to have to fit the whole bag, as well as be deep enough to hide it and not be found after the rain or if someone kicks up some dirt. They are going to be digging for a while.

Finally, after what seemed like forever, they had decided this was the best it was going to be. They dropped the bag into the hole, not before tearing a little hole into the bag so that there wouldn't be any air to cause any issues.

"Wait, before you start dropping the dirt back onto them. Should we say anything?" said Katrina.

Joey and Dustin looked at each other, then they looked at her. Then they looked back at each other and fell on the ground laughing.

"Ok assholes. Wouldn't you like someone to say something at your funeral?" said Katrina.

"Ha ha ha, I'm sorry baby. I am not laughing at you. It's just the thought of saying something about crows. Let me clear my throat. Ahem. Ok, here we go. I will say something. We gather here today to lay to rest, a murder of crows. That were murdered, in cold blood. They were placed on my yard into a pentagram in what seems to be a sacrificial ritual of some sorts. May they rest in peace....... ha ha ha ha ha. Ok, I can't keep it together," laughed Joey.

Katrina laughed, "Ok, ok. I get your point now. I guess that was pretty ridiculous. Well, anyway, get them buried before anyone comes to investigate why there are hyenas in the mountains laughing."

Joey and Dustin worked as fast as they could to fill up the dirt. They then went and grabbed some debris to try and cover up the freshly dug dirt. They grabbed as many fallen branches as they could. They also grabbed some leaves and whatever they could to make sure the dirt was naked to the visible eye. Satisfied with their work, they were ready to leave. They grabbed their shovels and headed back to the car. They tossed the shovels in the trunk and turned back around to head back to Joey and Katrina's.

Even though they just had a good laugh, the happiness was short lived. The worry and confusion quickly set back in as they were making their way back. The tension in the car started to rise again.

Dustin said, "What do you think happened to Brian?"

Joey looks in the rearview mirror, "I don't know. I really hope he's ok though. I am sure he was just pissed and sleeping it off. Or trying to recover in some sort of other way."

"Yea, I guess you're right. I am sure we will hear from him soon."

They traveled in silence the rest of the way home. When they arrived, they looked around to see if there was anything else out of the ordinary. They walked over to where the crows were laying on the yard, there were what looked like burn marks on the grass from the bodies. It wasn't like fire, it was like where each crow body was, it somehow destroyed the grass beneath it, leaving exposed dirt in the shapes of all of the bodies.

"Were they poisoned? Maybe there was so much poison in their systems it seeped through and killed the lawn. I guess something to think about," said Joey.

"Ok friends, well the time has come, I need to go home. I don't know how the fuck I am going to carry on with the days, but I have to go to work in a few hours. I will come by after work if that's ok. Text me if you hear from Brian at all," said Dustin.

Dustin then walked over to his carved-up car and took off for home. Joey and Katrina made their way inside so they could get cleaned up and take a much needed nap. They were hoping to hear from Brian, but they also wanted to get some much needed rest.

*****

Dustin made his way into work. He was going to be working from 2pm to 11pm. Dustin works as a manager in the local Lowes. Dustin was a good worker within his company. He also liked to keep his weirdness on the low while at work. Even though he would let things slip from time to time, he definitely didn't let his freak flag fly too high while at work; being in management, he had a standard to uphold. That particular day, when he got to work, he had felt that there was something off. Something didn't sit right with him, so he asked the manager that was going to be leaving if there was anything going on that he needed to know about. That manager just nodded their head, nothing out of the ordinary it seems.

As Dustin's shift went on, peculiar things started happening. First, it started with two crows that flew into the building and were flying around and sitting in-between the isles on top of the dividers. They would make obnoxious cawing as people walked by. Dustin felt odd about this due to just having to bury a mass of crows. He then had to attempt with another department manager to get the crows out, following them around with pool nets trying to catch them. Eventually, as they chased them around, they escaped through one of the doors.

Even though they had chased the crows out of the building, Dustin noticed that they were still sitting outside in the parking lot. Almost as if they were taunting him, watching him. Dustin thought he was starting to go a little crazy, well... crazier than usual being paranoid about crows watching him. After all, they were just crows, right? As the day continued, there were more things that started to happen that just didn't make sense. A customer had come up to Dustin and told him that there was an ant infestation on one of the isles.

Dustin thought that was odd, there was no way there could be an ant infestation. How would they get through the tile floor? Dustin took a trip over to the isle, sure enough, somehow an ant hill has made its way through the tile floor.

In the middle of the isle. A pretty big one that couldn't just pop up out of nowhere. So, thinking quickly on his feet, he blocked off the isle for the time being and called in an exterminator. Luckily, he found one that responds to emergency issues in businesses. The exterminator should be there within an hour or so. Should be problem solved for the night, right?

It is getting close to closing time and the exterminator should be there soon so they can get the ant issue taken care of. The night was about to change drastically. A man and woman walked into the store five minutes before close. They had an eerie stare on them. They didn't say anything to anyone and walked out of sight for a minute. The man emerged and went to the check-out area. Dustin was at the front, watching as the customers were making their final purchases. The man was up next to be rang up, but the odd thing was he didn't have any items with him.

Dustin took note of this and was keeping an eye on him, also glancing around to see if he could find where the woman had gone to. The man stepped up, turned away from the check stand to face the store, and at that point there was a noise in the nearby distance. It was the sound of a gas motor starting up. It was a chainsaw being cranked on. He then heard the chainsaw rev up and sound as if it was getting closer. The woman appeared, holding a chainsaw. Holding it up in the air. She ran directly at the man that she had come to the store with. She slammed the chainsaw into the man without hesitation.

The man was pointing at Dustin. The entire time he was being chopped into pieces, his hand was pointing at Dustin, well that was until she cut off his arm. He was looking directly at him as well, keeping eye contact. However, he never even showed an ounce of pain or acknowledgment of being sawed into pieces. After the final slice, putting the chainsaw directly down the middle of his head, the body, or what was left of it, finally went lifeless on the floor. There was blood everywhere. Splatters in every direction. A puddle quickly increasing on the floor.

There were still customers around the scene. Some sprayed with blood. No one could move. Everyone was frozen with fear, or maybe it was the work of something else. The woman got on her hands and knees, looking over to Dustin, making eye contact. With a smile so big it was eerie. She started to laugh uncontrollably. She never stopped looking at Dustin now. Drawing some sort of symbols. Once she had completed the symbols, she stood up and grabbed the chainsaw again. The entire store was silent, not knowing what was going to happen next. Everyone just watches the woman's every move. She raised the chainsaw into the air again, revving up the engine. She proceeded to run the chainsaw to the left side of her neck. Making sure that it was going to continue to run all the way through her body slicing it in half by the momentum. Partially through, the body fell to the ground. Although it did not fully complete cutting all the way through, the chainsaw was on top of the mangled corpse still sending chunks of flesh flying throughout the nearby vicinity.

When she was finally dead, it was as if the trance on everyone was ended. The screams started, the panic and running around. Dustin grabbed his cell phone and called 911. The police were there fast. Getting everyone's statements, but the problem was, no one knew how to even explain what they had witnessed. The other part of it was that everyone had told the police how both people were pointing and looking at Dustin when the unspeakable catastrophe was happening.

The police came to Dustin to question him, first as the manager of the store. Second, as the person who was being singled out by the — well they aren't victims, they are considered the conspirators —.

The police officer asked, "Sir, do you know these people?"

Dustin answered, "No sir, I have never seen them before a day in my life."

"Uh, huh. Can you explain why everyone said they were looking and pointing at you the whole time?"

"That's because they were doing that. That doesn't mean I know who they are. I am actually really freaked out about this. Can you tell me who they were? Why were they targeting me?"

"Calm down now. I am the one asking the questions, ok?"

"Ok."

"What do you know of these people? Have they been in here before?"

"I just told you; I have no idea who they are. I have never seen them before. I don't even understand at all."

"Uh huh. So, you are telling me, there is no connection to you? They just came in here and singled you out for no reason?"

"What the fuck? I already told you; I have no idea who they are or what they wanted with me. I don't understand why you are asking me this when I have already answered you. Aren't you supposed to be making me feel better or something? Fuck."

"Whoa, whoa, whoa. No need to get violent with your words here. I am just checking every which way I can. Maybe we will have to speak to you later, when you can recollect yourself. Thank you, sir, for your time. I hope you find some peace within yourself and if you think of anything else, here is my card."

The police officer handed Dustin his business card. Dustin rolled his eyes and put the card into his pocket. This situation had gone from bad to worse to off the hinge. Dustin took care of all the things he needed to take care of before he could leave, he was management after all and there was a business to run. Mangled bodies or no mangled bodies. The police took care of getting the clean-up crews that will be coming to handle the corpses and blood. The time, well, the time of night was irrelevant at this point. Dustin didn't care and had to go to Joey's and let them know exactly what had just happened.

Dustin sped over to Joey's and realized that it had to be pretty late. All the lights were off within the house, that only happened when it was really late in the night. Dustin went into the backyard and went to the back door of the garage, where he proceeded to knock. He knocked... and knocked... and knocked. Gradually getting louder with every knock. At this point, he wasn't sure if he was starting to get worried why they weren't answering or if it was just that late that it was hard for them to wake up.

Dustin decided to say fuck it and tried to open the door. He grabbed the handle and continued to turn the knob. No luck here either, the door was locked. Just then, the door handle jiggled from the other side, after hearing the deadbolt twisted to release. Joey opened the door and looked at Dustin with squinting eyes.

"Hey man, what are you doing here so late?" asked Joey.

"You have no idea what just happened to me at work. Can I come in and tell you?" replied Dustin.

"Yea man, come on in. You don't look so good anyway."

Dustin came into the room, he couldn't sit, he was pacing back and forth. Joey went back to his bed where Katrina was laying under the covers.

Dustin said, "You are going to want to wake up Katrina for this one. It's so crazy. It doesn't even make any sense at all."

Joey nodded his head, looked over to Katrina and started to lightly shake her arm. She just pushed off his hand grumbling. Joey continued to do so while increasing the intensity slightly until she acknowledged she was being woken up. Not realizing they had company, Katrina slept in the nude whenever they were alone, she hopped up out of bed to go to the bathroom.

"Ahhhhh, what the fuck Dustin. What are you doing here?" said Katrina.

Dustin turned around quickly, "Sorry Katrina, I came here to tell you guys some crazy shit that just happened. It was too important to wait."

Katrina said, "Ok. I'm going to go pee really quick."

Katrina walked over to the bathroom and went inside. She still didn't have any clothes on but walked back to the bed and got under the covers. Dustin proceeded to tell them the story about what had happened to him. Joey and Katrina were no longer tired and were looking at Dustin in disbelief.

"What the fuck does this even mean? It is obviously from them. But how did they control these people to make them do that to themselves?" asked Joey.

"You should've seen their faces as they were just staring at me. They were pointing at me. I have never been so scared in my life. I felt like they were marking me for something. It did not feel good at all. Whatever it is, it is not good."

Dustin stayed over for the night; they didn't speak much after what was discussed between them. It was more of a type of hypnosis; them all being stuck in shock of the situation. They eventually nodded off, only to worry about what's next to come and they would individually jump awake every so often.

Chapter 14

Morning finally came, Dustin was the first to wake, he was sleeping on the couch. His eyes were partially open, still having the sleep stuck on his eyelashes. Only he saw a figure standing above him. It was the silhouette of a man, more of a shadow. He opened his eyes completely, and the figure was gone.

Dustin jumped up and yelled, "What the fuck was that? Who was that? Where did he go?"

Joey and Katrina both sat up in a fright.

"What? What are you talking about? What the fuck is going on?" said Joey.

"There was like a dark figure standing over me when I woke up. When I fully opened my eyes though, he was gone. Jesus Christ, what the fuck is going on?" yelled Dustin.

"I didn't see anything when I sat up, but I guess that's when you said it was already gone. Did you already check the bathroom?" asked Joey.

Dustin nodded his head no, then walked over to the bathroom as fast as he could. He stuck his head into the bathroom, nothing, he moved the curtain from the bathtub, nothing. There was no one or no thing within the room. The door was still locked, nothing could've come in, nothing could've left.

"I don't know what to tell you, I mean, my parents always joked the house was haunted Maybe it doesn't have anything to do with what's going on. Hey, have you heard from Brian? I have been trying to get ahold of him. He seems to be off the face of the earth," said Joey.

"Fuck, of course it's fucking haunted. Your house wouldn't be your house if it wasn't fucking haunted. No, I haven't heard from him. He might really be freaked out after drinking that blood, or should I say being force fed it. You can't really blame him after that situation. He will come around eventually." said Dustin.

Joey was going to have to go to work today, even after all the madness. Joey worked in the local Vons grocery store. He was a Produce Clerk. His shift today was going to be from 12pm-9pm. Joey realized that it was about to be

10am, he knew he had to get up and start getting ready for work.

"Hey man, you're welcome to stay, but I have to get ready for work now. My shift starts at 12. I am just going to eat and take a shower," said Joey.

"No, it's ok. I am going to go home and try to get more sleep anyway. This has all been too much. See you guys later. Hit me up if you talk to Brian, I will do the same," said Dustin.

Joey got up and made his way to the bathroom to take a shower, Katrina decided she wanted to partake in the shower as well. Dustin had just left when Joey had already stepped in the shower, Katrina stayed to lock the door before heading to the shower. She locked the door and stripped down to go join in. As she was walking towards the bathroom, it sounded like the door handle was being opened, but furiously. She ran back to the door, unlocked it and opened it slightly so she could speak out in case Dustin was there. There was no one there. She closed the door, thinking maybe she was just imagining it. She locked it again and started to walk away, again the handle was rattling. This time she was still right by the door. She looked at it as the handle was moving, she unlocked the door and swung it open thinking Dustin was playing a trick. No one was there.

Now getting spooked, she slammed the door shut and locked it. She didn't wait to see if it would do the same thing again. She ran straight to the bathroom and hopped into the shower. She hugged Joey.

"Whoa, hey now. Are you ok? Your heart is beating so fast," asked Joey.

"The doorknob was shaking like someone was trying to open the door. I opened it and no one was there. The moment I closed it and locked it again, the handle did the same thing. I opened it while it was still moving, no one was there. I thought maybe Dustin was playing a trick on us, but there was no one there," answered Katrina.

"Fuck. This isn't good. First Brian was attacked and force-fed blood. Then Dustin had that crazy shit at his work, now you're being scared with the doorknob shaking," said Joey.

"Well, when you put it like that, at least it was only the doorknob. I guess it could've been a lot worse."

"I wasn't even thinking of it like that, but yea it definitely could've been a lot worse."

Joey and Katrina took their shower. When they got out, they went to the room to get dressed and the room was incredibly cold. It felt as if it was freezing temperatures. They were immediately shivering. They just looked at each other with concern, not saying anything. They threw on their clothes and stepped into the backyard. The backyard was warm, the sun was out. They stepped back into the room, and it was no longer cold as ice.

"Ok Katrina, when I go to work, maybe you should take the car and do something. Go to a store, don't stay at home alone," said Joey.

"Yea, I was kind of thinking the same thing. I can drop you off and I will just go to different places. I'll come back by on your lunch break, too," answered Katrina.

Joey and Katrina decided to leave a little early so they could grab a bite to eat. They decided on eating California's favorite burger place, In N Out. Joey got a double, double animal style, with animal fries. Katrina got just a cheeseburger with no tomato, regular onion, regular fries. They both got Arnold Palmer drinks with the pink lemonade of course.

It came time for Katrina to drop off Joey. She took him to work and dropped him off. Both were feeling a bit off about everything going on.

"Keep your phone on just in case I need to get ahold of you. Keep it by your side. If you need to get ahold of me right away, call the store. Love you, go to Barnes and Noble, read some books, enjoy your day. Love you," said Joey as he closed the door.

Joey walked inside the store and waved before entering. Katrina drove off and decided Joey was right. She would head over to Barnes and Noble. Maybe she could read up on spirits, or something of that nature. Maybe she could find some answers of what's going on, or at least something that might point them in some sort of direction.

Joey made his way over to the time clock, where he said hi and waved to all of the checkers that were working. Immediately, Joey had a weird feeling, something felt off. He didn't know what it was, but there was just something wrong. He shrugged and walked over to the produce section. He wasn't going to ignore the weird feeling, definitely going to be on high alert, but his shift still needed to go on.

Joey went behind the doors where there was the backroom for the produce section. There was another set of doors to the side that led to the cooler of all the back stock of fruits and vegetables. His manager was standing there at the little podium desk.

Joey said, "Hey, what's up man? How's everything going?"

Jim replied, "Hey Joey, it's another cluster fuck of a day. We have been slammed, and all the display tables have been getting ransacked. Alex called out this morning, so we've been shorthanded the whole time while getting called for checker service as well."

Joey raised his eyebrows, "That kind of day huh? Well, don't worry, I am here now, we will definitely get this stuff worked."

Jim nodded. Joey put on his apron, walked out to the sales floor and took note of what needed to be restocked first. The apple table seemed to be the lowest, so Joey walked back to the backroom and grabbed his cart and began to fill it up with the apples.

*****

Katrina made her way over to Barnes and Noble. She figured she could look in the occult section and see if there was anything that she could possibly find that might give them some sort of idea of what's going on. As Katrina parked the car and got out, she noticed that people seemed really angry. There was a mother walking with her son who was probably around 6; the mother was holding his wrist and pulling him along while yelling at him. She wasn't really saying much while yelling, just seemed to be mad at the world and taking it out on the poor kid.

There was an older man who was getting out of his truck that he had just parked. The only thing, before he could get out, a young guy had parked next to him. His car was too close to the old man's truck and would obviously have a hard time getting out. The old man visibly frustrated, opened his door. Only he opened it fast and hard, making sure he slammed it into the car next to him. He then repeatedly opened and closed his truck door making a large dent in the car's door.

The young guy jumped out of his car, "HEY! WHAT ARE YOU DOING? YOU'RE MESSING UP MY CAR!"

"YOU SHOULDN'T HAVE BLOCKED ME IN YOU INCONSIDERATE MOTHER FUCKER," the old man yelled.

Right after he yelled that, he closed his door and put the truck in reverse and slammed on the gas. The old man flew backwards in reverse as he turned the wheel. He then backed up into an innocent car. The old man didn't even hesitate to drive off at high speeds not even looking back to see what kind of damage he left to the unfortunate car. The old man sped off, the young guy watching in shock, almost not knowing what to do, shook his head and jumped back in his car to follow the old man.

Katrina was just standing by her car, looking around and wondering what could possibly happen next. She sat there for a minute and looked around to see if there was anyone else doing something crazy. So far, she seemed to be in the clear to proceed to her destination. She was being extra cautious of what was going on around her, especially after the wild interactions that were going on. Katrina made it to the front door of Barnes and Noble, so far so good. She made it into the store, she looked side to side, no one doing anything out of the ordinary.

"Ok, I think I might be alright," Katrina was thinking to herself.

Katrina made her way through the store to the back section where the occult books are located. It was hard to even think about what could possibly relate to their problem. Katrina found a couple of ghost books that she skimmed through. Nothing. There was a book about demons, nothing. A book about possession, ok, there might be something here. Katrina continued reading through the book, where things were starting to sound a little familiar. There were parts speaking about rituals to conduct a possession, this seemed too close for comfort.

Katrina was really starting to get into the book when she heard in the distance, there was some commotion. It sounded as if there was someone shouting. Katrina stopped what she was doing and tried to focus on the noise. There was a woman speaking very loudly. It was hard to hear what she was saying, so Katrina started to walk closer to where the noise was coming from. The woman went silent for a minute. The quiet minute felt as if it was lasting a lifetime, until she let out a blood curdling scream. Wailing at the top of her lungs. Throwing her arms around in circles, she turned towards where Katrina was.

Katrina was behind a bookshelf, not visible to the woman, but it was as if she could sense her there. The woman started grabbing the display books off the tables and throwing them towards Katrina. Throwing two at a time and as hard as she could. Some would fly over the top and land near Katrina, others would bounce off the other side of the bookshelves making a loud thud next to where Katrina was standing.

One of the booksellers walked up to the woman and tried to calm her down. The woman looked at her in the eyes, what seemed to be peering into her soul and trying to devour it from a look. The bookseller started to get uncomfortable after the woman went silent and didn't take her eyes off her. The manager ran to the phone and dialed 911.

The woman looked at the manager and said, "You are doomed."

The woman then turned her attention back to the bookseller and grabbed the two biggest hardcovers and smacked her across the face with one of them. The bookseller stumbled back while grabbing her face due to her nose erupting with blood. The woman smiled and hit her with the other book. The woman whacked her with the books repeatedly until she fell to the ground. That is when she unleashed many kicks to the side, her head, and stomping on the now limp body of the bookseller. Everyone within the store is stunned, not knowing what to do.

The woman continues to stomp on the head of the bookseller, there is an ever-growing pool of blood leaking out of the mouth, ears, and newly created holes on the side of her head. The manager dropped his phone, the 911 dispatcher is still on the phone, but it didn't matter at this point. He looked at the woman and let out a scream…well it was more of a screech. He rushed the woman and tackled her to the ground. Unfortunately, he reacted too late, the bookseller was dead.

After tackling her, he stood up and ran to the bookseller to see if she was still alive, this was by the customer service kiosk in the middle of the store. The woman stood up, looked over and grabbed the stapler that was sitting by the computers. She walked over to the manager, repeatedly smacking the stapler on the back of his head. Stapling over and over. She grabbed a paperback book that was on the counter, she looked at the cover, "New Witch in Town" by Michael Gregory II. She opened up the cover and laid it onto the top of his head. *Boom*, smacked the stapler several times so that the book would be fastened to the top of his head. The manager stayed on his knees, screaming, watching the blood drop off his face. He could feel the warm liquid running down each part of his body.

    The manager was frozen with fear and pain. The crazy woman, still with the stapler, decided that it was a good idea to staple the managers ears, giving him many piercings with the little staples hanging out. At this point, she was bored with the staples; it doesn't really do too much damage. She then grabbed two pens from the cup holder. Held them high into the air for extra theatrics and swung them down stabbing the manager in the sides of his body. Then she went on a stabbing spree and repeatedly stabbed him in different areas of his body. The manager probably didn't have much life left in him at this point, she dropped one of the pens, grabbed him by the hair, pulled his head back so his face is looking at the ceiling, and drove the pen all the way into his eye. There was no pen left, his body fell to the ground and started to convulse.

Everyone in the store was in complete shock, had no idea what to do, no idea how to react. The woman then looked over to Katrina once again, she pointed at her and laughed. Just then, the police came running into the store with their guns drawn.

"Put your fucking hands up!" yelled the police officers.

The woman, still looking and pointing at Katrina, takes off in a full sprint towards the police officers. Laughing the entire time, the police have no other option then to start shooting. They unload their clips into her. There was three police officers and they each shot until they were out of bullets. The woman was somehow still trying to crawl towards the police officers. She was bleeding, a lot. Crawling, she reached the first police officer and grabbed their leg. She bit the officer on the leg, he hit the back of her head with his pistol. She fell to the ground, still laughing, she looked over to Katrina again. She reached up to grab the officer again, this time one of the other officers had changed the magazine in their gun and shot her in the head. The body flopped to the ground. She was dead.

At this point, everyone had looked over to Katrina. Not saying anything, but everyone was wondering why the woman had targeted her, making it so apparent she was somehow connected to Katrina. The police officers continued to follow procedure and rounded up everyone for questioning.

******

Joey was working the produce tables, stocking them up as high as he could. Some of the apple tables were stocked so high that they were almost a full pyramid covering the price signs. One thing that Jim had said that was correct, was it being a madhouse, and they continuously kept getting called to the front for checker service. This was making it nearly impossible to get anything done.

"Joey, check stand service please," a woman's voice said over the intercom.

Frustrated, Joey shook his head as he walked away from his cart and headed towards the front to assist on the lines. Joey made it to the front where there were many people in lines ready to check out. He went to a register and clicked on the light, calling over whoever was next. The person who got into his line was a middle-aged mother with blonde hair, and two young kids with her. As Joey started to ring up the items from the conveyer belt, another person caught his eye. There was a man standing by the floral department, staring at him. Not moving, not blinking, just staring. He had a very peculiar look on his face, just blank.

Joey tried to just shake it off, maybe it was nothing and the guy was not deliberately staring at him directly. Joey continued to help the people that were in his line, when he continued to feel as if someone was staring at him. He looked up and noticed that the man did not move and indeed was staring straight at him. It was making him uncomfortable, but he didn't want to act like it was getting to him. Joey thought maybe if he ignored it long enough, the man would eventually lose interest and walk away.

That was not the case. The man gradually came closer to Joey's register. He eventually got directly into Joey's line. When it was his turn to be rung up, Joey looked up and saw the man with the same expression he had the entire time.

"Hi sir, how are you doing today?" said Joey.

The man did not change his expression, he turned around and faced the cashier in the register that was in front of him. There just so happens to be scissors sitting next to the cash register printer. The man picked them up and repeatedly stabbed the cashier in the back, shoulder, and neck. He must have stabbed the cashier 15 times before the cashier could even notice that it was happening. Blood was spraying out of the cashier's neck like a fountain. He slowly turned around and made eye contact with Joey.

Not being able to hold himself up anymore, the cashier fell backwards, and blood sprayed all over the register. The customer that was in his line was also doused in blood. The woman who was now wearing a crimson liquid cover started to scream. She couldn't move, just screamed. The attacker then turned his attention to the screaming woman. He grabbed the shopping cart to his side and picked it up and threw it at the woman. Everyone was shocked at this, shopping carts are heavy and awkward, they should not be handled this easily.

The woman was hit by the shopping cart and bounced backwards into the check stand behind her. Now her own blood was spurting out of her face, her forehead, nose, and lips were split. Without hesitation, the man jumped over the check stand that had the now corpse occupying it. He grabbed the chords that were attached to the printer and wrapped them around the woman's neck. He turned and faced Joey, leaning forward as the chords went over his shoulder and he was hoisting the woman up by her neck on his back. It didn't take long until the woman's kicking stopped, and the body went limp. Once again, everyone was frozen in fear, except Joey. He finally snapped out of it and ran out of his check stand.

He ran straight to the man, there just so happen to be a fire extinguisher at the front help desk. Joey grabbed it and rushed the man, slamming it into his head. The guy laughed, he fell back hard but laughed. The man was in the middle of the check-out isle now, starting to stand up, Joey ran at him and punt kicked him to the face as hard as he could. Blood sprayed from his nose and mouth. He laughed again and started to stand up. Joey grabbed the fire extinguisher once again and smacked the man several times across the head. He did it repeatedly until the man went limp. He was still alive, but unconscious now. Joey quickly grabbed some zip ties that he carried in his apron and tied the man's hands and legs up behind him in the traditional hog tie. To keep him from doing any more harm before the police showed up.

The man was bleeding from the wounds inflicted by Joey, but they weren't that bad. Nothing near what he would deserve, some might say in comparison of what he had just inflicted. The man started to wake while they were waiting for the police to arrive. He was looking around, and looked directly at Joey, then the devilish grin returned. He started smacking his own head on the ground.

"I may have failed in killing more, but there is one left to die before the police get here," the man said.

"What? What the fuck are you talking about?" asked Joey.

Katrina came running into the store and Joey caught eye of her. He looked up and was wide eyed, she looked at him with the same reaction. She stopped in her tracks and looked around, then saw the man on the ground, as well as the bodies in the check stands.

"Joey! What is going on?" screamed Katrina.

Katrina ran to Joey and squeezed him with a passionate hug, hoping that his embrace will somehow make all the pain go away.

As Katrina grabbed ahold of Joey, the man screamed with laughter. Violently slamming his head into the ground, rocking himself up to get extra force. His head started to leak more and more blood while splattering everything within the nearest four-foot vicinity. He managed to rock himself up to his knees, where he somehow created enough force to snap the zip ties that were holding him together. Within a few seconds, he was free. He jumped up on top of the check stand, reached down and grabbed a pen. He jumped at full force to get maximum height and proceeded to dive to the floor while placing the pen point directly at his eye. It appeared to be in slow motion, but it was only a few seconds. The man was dead. He landed forehead first on the ground, completely vertical. The pen logged into his eyeball, and sinking all the way in, disappearing behind his now exploded eyeball. The man's neck snapped, as well as where he was smacking his head on the ground had now split in two. Blood and brain matter splashed on the floor while puddles of blood formed.

Katrina was in shock after going from one wild tragedy to another. The police had arrived and came storming in guns drawn. When they realized that there was no more threat, they put their guns down and started asking questions.

When they looked at Katrina, one officer asked, "Weren't you just at the crime scene at Barnes and Noble?"

"Yes, I was. It was awful." said Katrina.

"Wait what? Crime scene? What happened? Are you ok?" asked Joey.

"I will tell you all about it, we need to get ahold of Dustin. Some bad shit is going on. Let's just finish talking to these police officers and get the fuck out of here."

Chapter 15

Joey and Katrina got ahold of Dustin the next day. Dustin was sleeping all day after his wild incident the night before. Unbeknownst to what was going on throughout the city with his friends, he received a text from Joey in the morning saying it was urgent to come over. So, naturally, he made his way over as quickly as possible.

After arriving at Joey and Katrina's place, he was hurried inside and brought to the couch. Joey then proceeded to explain to him what had happened to him, as well as Katrina explained what happened to her.

"What the fuck guys. Obviously, this is not a coincidence. All three of us have witnessed someone killing people and then killing themselves. Not only just doing the damn thing, but in a very brutal fashion,." said Dustin.

"I know. This isn't good. Where the fuck has Brian been, too? I haven't heard anything form him in a long time. Have you heard from him Dustin?" asked Joey.

"Nope. Not a peep., answered Dustin.

"Obviously everything we have been experiencing is connected. This all started when we were at that cemetery. We saw the cult people. It has to do with them. I am sure of it. So what the fuck do we do?" asked Katrina.

"I think we need to go back there. I think we need to try and explore the cemetery, or maybe even the cult house that is right there. I don't know. This is fucked up, and really dangerous. I don't know how much more dangerous it could get though, there are people being possessed or something and killing innocents and themselves," said Joey. "So I guess it's decided, we need to go to the cemetery again. We need to check it out. Look for something. Try to figure anything out, we can't have all these people getting killed around us. The police won't be any help either, they are either in the cult or they are paid off by them. This is a fucked up situation."

"Yea, this is really fucked up," said Dustin. "This is some real bull shit. I wish we never would've gone to that damn place."

"We can't change the past so we just have to do what we can. We have to go back. I don't know what we are going to do there, but we have to figure out something. Otherwise I am afraid of what might happen to one of us. I mean, what ever happened to Brian anyway?" said Joey. "Should we just go tonight? Say fuck it, go on a recon mission and see what we can spy on from afar? Let's get some sort of binoculars or something. Or maybe a video camera with a good zoom or something. What say you?"

Katrina nodded her head; she almost always agrees to Joeys wild ideas.

"We really don't have much of another choice anyway," answered Dustin.

"Ok then, I guess it's settled. We go tonight and see if there is anything else going on there," said Joey.

The three of them sat there, conversing, not a lot. Very infrequent, still in shock from everything.

"Maybe we should eat and do something to try and take our minds off of what we are doing tonight," suggested Katrina.

"What could we do?" asked Joey.

"I don't know, maybe let's play some Mario Kart?" said Katrina.

Dustin and Joey both nodded their heads in agreement.

"Now for a very important question, what do you want to eat? I suggest pizza," said Joey.

Dustin and Katrina both nodded their heads in excited agreement. Joey grabbed his phone and continued to place the order. They were ordering from Blaze Pizza, so they each individually made a pizza sculpted to their own personalized perfection. The three of them played Mario Kart until the delivery driver arrived with their pizzas. Ordering on the delivery apps is way too convenient, not even having to speak to the driver when they drop off the order.

They all grab their pizzas and sit down, now having to deal with thinking again instead of taking their mind off of the situation by playing video games. While sitting, they each were starting to think a little too much. Joey recognized that the others looked to be getting stressed by the second in thought.

"Hey, why don't we watch something? Maybe we can watch a show that can relate to our situation, something like Supernatural?" said Joey.

"Why not, who knows, maybe we can get some ideas from it," answered Dustin.

Joey and Dustin both look to Katrina, "Yea, that sounds like a great idea," said Katrina.

They could only take so much of watching the show and eating trying to ignore their immediate situation.

"So, I guess we need to figure out what we are going to take with us so we can look from afar. Maybe we should get a video camera with good zooming. That way we can film it and have proof," said Joey.

"Yea, I think that's a good idea. Let's go to Best Buy and get a video camera. Besides, I have a hookup there and we can get a good price," said Dustin.

The three of them closed their pizza boxes and put them in the refrigerator. Besides having name tags on the boxes from the delivery order, they each knew their pizzas, as they were completely different from each other's. They then walked out to Joey's car and got in. They made their way down to Best Buy and parked. Sitting in silence as they wait for one another to make the first move of getting out of the parked car. Not really thinking or saying anything about it, but they were all getting a little spooked thinking about their own individual situations that they all just went through.

"Alright, I guess I'll make the first move. Let's get out and get this camera," said Joey.

Without saying a word, Dustin and Katrina just agreed and followed. Slowly, they all made their way into the store. Shuffling their feet, trying to prolong the inevitable, they reach the video camera section. Looking at each, wanting to make sure that there is going to be a good zoom, as well as works good in low light. Sure enough, they find one that fits all their criteria. This camera is expensive, however they think it is of upmost importance, and get it.

"Well, I guess there's that problem solved, now we can see what's going on when we are there," said Dustin.

Once again, the three of them go silent for the rest of the trip and make their way back to the garage. Without saying a word to each other, they bring in the video camera, plug it in to make sure it's charged. For the rest of the day, they basically stay quiet while moving around the room, pacing, not sure what to do. Even though it feels as if it is moving in slow motion, the time passes and is late at night.

"Wow, where did the time go? I swear we just got back from the store and the rest is a blur," said Katrina.

"Well, I guess the time has come. We are going back to the cemetery. So... Ok, I am just trying to lag our time," said Joey. "Fuck it. Let's just do the damn thing. How else are we going to help our town?"

The three of them make their way to Joey's car. Katrina gets in shotgun, Dustin in the back with the camera. Joey to the driver's seat. Just sitting there, they each take a deep breath and slowly let it out before Joey starts up the car. Slowly, he starts to pull away from the front of his home. No music, no talking. Just silence. The ride to the cemetery is not a far one.

They pull up to the same parking spot they park at every time. This time, something seemed off, more than usual at least. They all get out of the car, make their way to the wall and hop over. Again, something seemed off. Quiet, really quiet. Everything, even nature was silent. It was eerie. It didn't make any sense. The energy in the air didn't feel quite right. Still, they decided they were there for one reason and they were going to complete this mission. Besides, they were only there for reconnaissance, what could possibly go wrong?

They started to make their way through the nursery, in which once again, silence. No security, no sounds, nothing. They make it to the gate of the cemetery, almost as if a path has been crafted for them. It was possibly their easiest excursion yet.

"Ok, we are here now. Where should we go to try and spy on the house?" asked Dustin.

"Did you guys think that might have been just a little too easy to get here? Something seems off," said Katrina.

"I don't really know Dustin, maybe we should go to the top inside the cemetery and try to film down towards the house. Now that you mention it. Katrina, that did seem a little too easy. Let's just hope that was some sort of coincidence," said Joey.

They enter through the gate and start to make their way to the top. As they do so, there are noises rustling throughout the bushes amongst the surrounding gate walls.

"You hear that? Now the animals are finally starting to move around," said Katrina. "Kind of odd that it didn't start until now."

They reached the top of the cemetery. Luckily, they had a clear line of sight towards the cult house. Dustin turned on the camera and aimed it in that direction. He zoomed in, he didn't use the viewer screen, they didn't want to have any extra light emission from the camera to show where they were. Dustin looked through the viewer and zoomed, he scrolled around looking to see if he could see anything.

"Holy fucking shit! I guess we came on the right night!" Dustin whispered excitedly. "They have something going on in their backyard. There are a bunch of people standing in a circle wearing robes. There is a girl standing in the middle. Look."

Katrina jumped to the camera before Joey could. She grabbed and aimed in the direction where Dustin said to look. What Katrina then saw was something she didn't even want to tell them.

"Oh my god. They dropped their robes. All of them are naked. The girl in the middle is holding a chalice. She just dumped it on herself, it's red. Oh fuck, I think it's blood," Katrina shrieked and handed the camera to Joey.

"What the fuck. They are all biting her now. It looks like they are eating her. She's standing, and they are all ravishing her while tearing her flesh off, piece by piece. This is disturbing. It looks like there are several circles of this happening all at once. I think we got what we needed. Let's get the fuck out of here," said Joey.

Joey, Karina, and Dustin make their way back to the car. This appeared to be a job well done. They went and got exactly what they were looking for, and without getting caught or having any trouble. They still couldn't seem to feel any better about it though. What they witnessed will leave a scar on their soul after all. They plan on bringing the tape to the police the next day, even to the city hall to try and show the mayor. It is obvious there is something wrong going on. They get back and run inside.

"This was too easy. It was as if they almost just let us get what we wanted. It didn't make any sense. I guess we will just have to take the win and carry on. Tomorrow, we expose those rotten mother fuckers," said Joey.

Chapter 16

Even though they all did not sleep much, they got up bright and early. Well, early to them, which was eight am. They jumped up and grabbed the camera so they could run to the police station. They didn't even care about eating, drinking, brushing their teeth. Nothing. They just immediately ran to the car so they could get to the police station as fast as they could.

They got to the police station, where they went running in and ran straight to the window.

"Excuse me! Excuse me! We need to speak to the police chief right away. This is extremely important," yelled Joey.

"Hold on, sir. Can you please calm down? Let me know what it is you need to speak to him about," the police clerk responded.

"We have a tape that exposes a cult in upper Glendora that is killing people. It is so important that we speak to him."

"Wow, ok. Go sit down and I will go talk to him and see what he says."

She walks briskly to the back and disappears for a while. She then came out from the back with a concerned look on her face. She sits down instead of saying anything to them.

"Ok, that's weird. Did you guys see that? She just came out and sat down and has a look on her face like there is something wrong," said Joey.

The door from which the clerk had come from flew open. There was a tall man, older, strong demeanor and walking with purpose. His eyes lock on the three of them, in which he doesn't waiver, he doesn't even blink. There is a concerned look on his face, a bead of sweat starting to form at the top of his forehead.

"Hi there kids, I am the police chief you were asking for. Now, I was already briefed a little bit on what it is you wanted to talk to me about. Do you have evidence of these so-called cult members?" said the police chief.

"Yes, we do," Joey said calmly.

"Is that right?" said the police chief. "Well, that's unfortunate. You see here kids, these people you speak of are very dangerous people. My best advice to you is that you forget you ever knew any of this at all. Hope that they are willing to leave you alone for the rest of your life. There is a good chance that they won't, but if you are blessed by the lord and pray for forgiveness, only then you might have a slight chance of survival. You see, these people are everywhere. They have infiltrated the police department, hell they have infiltrated the damn government. They run it...They run everything."

Baffled. No one knows how to respond to what they just heard. Complete and utter failure.

"So, you're telling me that there is absolutely nothing the police can do to stop these murders and mutilations going on? What's the point in even having police then? What in the actual fuck?" Joey frustratedly said.

"Now hey, I was kind enough to let you know what's going on because I don't want to end up seeing your bodies in the next incident. I don't want to have that on my conscience. So once again, leave this alone because there is nothing I can do about it," the police chief exclaimed.

They got up without saying another word and immediately walked to the car. They get in the car, and Joey peels out of the police station parking lot. He floors it and speeds his way through downtown and pulls over when he is to the corridors in front of the ice cream shop.

"Ok, I used to think we were fucked before. But now that we know these people run everything, what the fuck are we supposed to do? They control the police chief and who knows what else. For all we know they control the government as well. I guess it is up to us to try and save the city. I guess the whole world at this point, ha ha ha. Wow, we are incredibly fucked," Joey said defeatedly.

Dustin lifts his head that he was laying on the back of the seats, "I guess we have no choice. They have our names, our addresses, fuck they probably know when we take a shit. Let's kill these fuckers. We will have to attack them at their next meeting. We are going to have to make this big though. We will have to figure out a way to take them all out. It will have to be at the cemetery. I'm thinking guns, fire, grenades, whatever we can get our hands on."

"You're not wrong... Why us? Why couldn't we have just continued our boring lives of watching horror movies and getting fucked up? This has been insane. I don't even know what to think about it at all. I hope you know someone, Dustin, that we can get our fire power from. My guess is that they will meet on the next full moon. That's in like one week. We have a whole week to prepare this shit," emphasized Katrina.

"Well, that is where our luck has turned. I do know someone. I have a hookup that will be able to get us things that can really do some damage. The best part is that it will all be illegal shit that can't be traced. The bad part is it's going to cost us a lot. The other thing, have you two ever shot a gun?" said Dustin.

Katrina shook her head no. Joey answered, "Well, I have shot a shotgun before. I am actually pretty good with a shotgun."

"Ok, well we will need at least two shotguns for you. I will get a shotgun, a couple handguns, and we will ask my buddy what kind of fire power we can get that will potentially have to take out an army. He will laugh at me, but this is no joke. Let's gather all the funds we can get. I will get as much as I can. Katrina, I will try to find something you can carry on you for a weapon. Maybe a machete or something that you can have better control of," said Dustin.

As soon as they got back to Joey's, Dustin left to gather whatever money he could come up with. Joey and Katrina went and pulled out all the money they had in their bank accounts. They then went back to their home and Joey made the decision he was going to raid inside and see if he could find any hidden money of his parents or brothers. He figured this would be warranted if any time to have to borrow said money without an explanation. He knew it would be better to ask for forgiveness than to ask for permission in this case.

Dustin sent Joey a text that said he got ahold of his buddy and will be set to meet tomorrow so there is plenty of time to try and gather as much as possible.

Chapter 17

The new day has come, the day that the group is going to get all the fire power they can get and prepare for killing many people. Something they have never even considered before. Here they are though, in an incredibly fucked up situation. Dustin showed up to their door and knocked, he also texted right before he got there so they wouldn't freak out from someone knocking on the door. Katrina opened the door and greeted Dustin.

"What's up man. Here's all we could pull together. It's around, three-thousand-dollars," said Joey.

"Nice, I was able to get twelve-hundred. So let's see what I can pull together. It is a friend, so I am hoping to get the homie discount. I will try to explain the circumstances that we are facing, but like I said before, I don't think he's going to believe me," said Dustin.

Dustin grabbed the money and left. Joey and Katrina sat back down and wondered what they should do to pass the time. There is so much tension and worry you could feel in the room. It was heavy. They decided that they were going to sit in bed and try to watch something light, maybe something that can lift their spirits. Some sort of comedy movie. Joey and Katrina then nod off while watching the movie for some much-needed rest.

They wake up to knocking at the door. Startled, Joey jumps up and is still a little wobbly. He is looking around, dazed and confused, not really remembering what is going on at the moment. He then gains his senses and walks over to the door and opens it. To add to his confusion, there is actually no one at the door. Now Joey is getting concerned, especially with the meeting they had with the police chief.

Dustin comes walking around the corner holding what appears to be two packed duffle bags.

"What took so long to answer the door? I was standing there and knocking for a while. Were you guys getting jiggy with it?" Dustin laughs.

"Ha ha, no we nodded off, I guess. Then we woke to you knocking. It actually startled us. So, did you get what we needed?" answered Joey.

"I got as much as I possibly could. He definitely gave me a good deal. I am surprised at how much I got. Let's just hope it's going to be enough. I'll show you what I got when we get inside."

They go inside the garage and close the door and lock it. Dustin walks to the center of the room and drops the bags. He proceeds to open them and starts pulling out an arsenal of weapons. There appears to be three semi-automatic shotguns, four handguns, several grenades, and a small handgun for Katrina, not to mention the large amount of ammunition. It would appear to be a lot of artillery, but they each are still secretly hoping that it will be enough. After all they have witnessed from these people, it is almost impossible to predict what they are capable of.

After the excitement has worn off from them having these weapons, they take a seat finally ready to discuss what and when they will be going to war.

"Ok, let's get a little recap on some things of what we know about these people. First, they have control over spirits, or can make zombies, or who knows what the fuck that is. Second, they control some living people too, making them do some diabolical shit. They have some sort of political involvement where some police officers are working for them directly, and the whole station won't do anything either. So basically, they are untouchable by the law. Well shit, when I put it all out there what the fuck are we thinking? Ha ha ha, they are damn near invincible," said Joey.

"In all reality, I don't know if we could really come up with a plan that would come close to being prepared for what's going to happen. I think what we should do is just grab all our stuff, go to the cemetery early, and then just camp out and hope for the best. Of course, we can create small plans with what we do in certain scenarios, but like I said, it will be damn near impossible to get fully prepared," said Dustin.

"I agree. I guess we will have to just do like we do with just about everything, wing it," said Katrina.

The group decided they were going to pack the guns and weaponry now and then they would be heading to the cemetery. There was no hesitation, after their conversation they were ready to leave. They decided it would be a good idea to pack a few bottles of alcohol, depending on preference. They knew they definitely needed to be somewhat intoxicated in order to do whatever it was they were going to be doing tonight. Obviously, they knew they couldn't get completely obliterated. They would need to be coherent enough to be able to operate their firearms. They take a couple of swigs of an open bottle of Makers Mark that was in the freezer before they head out.

On their way to the cemetery, they started to get a scary feeling. It was building as they got closer. They were all feeling it, but no one wanted to say anything. In what seemed to be a flash, they were already there and parking. It was as if they were in a trance and made it there without even realizing it. This time, they had to be a little more cautious about parking. They couldn't park in their normal spot because they didn't want to alarm the people who live right next to it. So, they decided to park in the middle of the community where there is guest parking. That would be less inconspicuous Joey had thought.

Now that they parked and grabbed their stuff, which seemed a lot bigger taking it out of the car than it did putting it in. They walked to where they hop over the wall and took one last look around to make sure no one was looking at them. Once they were satisfied with being in the clear, they quickly tossed the stuff over and hopped over faster than they ever had. A new problem had popped into their heads as soon as they hit the ground.

"I didn't think of this before, but what do we do if we see the security that is patrolling?" asked Katrina.

"Shit. Well, I guess we run and hide. I am not sure, I guess we will have to play it by ear," answered Joey.

The three of them continued on to make their way to the cemetery. Looking around, they couldn't see a single patrol car or security. It was as if this was already in place for them to be able to walk right in. Almost as if it was a trap. They made it to the entrance with ease. It was as simple as taking a stroll through the park.

So naturally, they began to get wearier of the situation that is unfolding before them.

"Well, that was oddly easy to get here. Let's go set up our stuff I guess and stash some things around. Then we can sit down, have a drink or two, and start to get some sort of game plan together. That way, we can at least try to be on top of everything. We can at least have somewhat of an idea of what we will be doing and how to possibly react to certain circumstances," suggested Joey.

Katrina and Dustin both agreed. So that was exactly what they did, they opened their bags and began to get fully prepared for what is to come. The guns that were meant for Katrina, Dustin handed to her. They also had shoulder holsters for each of them. One's that have spaces to put extra clips, shotgun shells, and two pistols. Joey has two shotguns, one with a built-in strap to carry on his back while carrying the other one. Dustin also has the same shotgun.

They all have their guns now in place with all the ammo they can carry with them. They grab the grenades, yes grenades. They put two on each of their shoulder holsters. They also strategically put a few around the cemetery in case they run out of ammo or lose their guns somehow as a fail-safe. After an hour or so of getting prepared, they start to feel pretty good about what they have accomplished in such a short period of time. Now they figured it was time to get a celebratory drink, especially because it is getting close to sundown, and they would likely need a little liquid encouragement.

"Cheers guys, it's been nice knowing you and hopefully we make it through whatever is going to happen tonight," Dustin depressingly said.

"Way to keep the spirits up Dustin," replied Joey.

"Just keeping it one *hunnit*," Dustin said, then laughed at his own slang.

They chuckled with Dustin.

"I actually find this hilarious that we are all geared up looking like suburban commando's. Who would've thought that us partiers would be the ones going to war with some kind of cult or evil force taking over our town," said Katrina.

They all raised their drinks and clanked them together.

"I think it's kind of funny that we are probably about to commit several murders. Will it count if they are possessed or ghosts or whatever they are? There seemed to be different kinds of things. I guess it doesn't really matter being that the police seem to stay completely out of it anyway. Here's to becoming serial killers," Joey laughed, while raising his glass again.

The eerie feeling of the cemetery grew as the sun was going down. It is now night-time and they continued to drink. Not too fast, because they didn't want to get wasted when they would need to have their reactions up to speed. Time was moving slow for them, the anticipation making them all restless. Not knowing what might be in store for them.

Finally, after a while of what felt like a lifetime of waiting for something to happen, there was movement starting to happen. There were noises coming from the nursery, silhouettes and shadows moving at the distant cult house.

"I guess things are about to get started. Whatever happens, I'm happy that we got to spend this time together," Joey said.

Dustin took a big swig of his bottle; Katrina took a deep breath and was shaking her body to free her nerves. They kneeled down and tried to hide themselves the best they could. That's when they saw that there were people starting to come into the cemetery entrance. That's when they heard a familiar voice.

"What exactly do you guys think you are doing?" asked Brian.

"Holy shit!" They all shrieked in unison.

"Where have you been? What happened to you? What the fuck are you doing now?" asked Joey.

"Don't worry, you will all be in the same place as me soon. I was born again that night. When they gave me the sacred juice of the gods, I was converted, and my eyes were opened. You see, they fed me the red nectar, and then they found me a few days later and delivered me in a ceremony," said Brian. "It doesn't hurt too much surprisingly. After that, when it's all over and you are reborn, nothing hurts anymore."

"Wait, does that mean they killed you? Did whatever they did to that one girl?" asked Dustin.

"Like I said, I was reborn again..... HEY! WE HAVE SOME VISITORS HERE. THEY CAN BE NEW RECRUITS." Brian yelled.

"Oh fuck, what did you just do to us Brian?" said Katrina.

Without hesitation, Joey took his shotgun and hit Brian as hard as he could in the back of the head, knocking him unconscious.

"Run. Get to the top and we will have to defend ourselves at the top of the hill," Joey directed.

The three of them did just that, leaving Brian's unconscious body where he had awkwardly landed. At the top of the hill, they turned around and looked down to see what they were going to have to deal with. What they saw was something they were not expecting. There were so many people making their way up to them. All of them concentrating on the three of them like there was nothing else in the world that mattered. As they started to look at them coming up the hill, they started to notice that some of them were already wounded or at least appeared to be. Deep cuts, but no blood coming out. It was as if they were almost zombies.

The only thing with them was that they were talking and communicating with each other. So, if they were zombies, they were sophisticated.

"It's now or never guys. Start blasting and don't hold back," said Joey.

"ADRIAAAAAANNNNNNNN," Dustin screamed in his best Rocky impersonation.

Dustin started blasting his shotgun into the ever-growing crowd that is making their way towards them. Joey grabbed a grenade, pulled the pin, and threw it as far as he could where it landed in the middle of the giant group.

"Merry Christmas....Ya filthy animal," Joey said right as the grenade went off sending bodies through the air. Many limbs, heads, and torsos flying in different directions. Blood spraying the ones far enough to not be hit with the blast, but close enough to be hit by the aftermath. The three of them continued to shoot their weapons knocking down front line after front line. Unfortunately, they just kept coming. They seemed to be an unstoppable force. This time, the three of them grabbed a grenade all together and threw the three grenades at the same time. A much bigger blast, and a much bigger tsunami of body parts went flying in every direction.

"Fuck, they keep coming. I swear the ones we shot are eventually getting back up and coming back after us," said Joey. "I think we need to run away. Let's hop the fence and run for it. I don't think we will survive if we stand our ground."

Joey helps Katrina jump over the fence. He nods to Dustin to hop over as well. Right when Joey turns and starts to climb the fence, his leg is grabbed. Dustin puts his shotgun through the chain-link fence, only a few inches from the face of the person grabbing his friend and pulls the trigger. The face and head of the man was blown in every which way possible. Chunks of hair, blood, brains, and fragments landed all over the place. Joey jumped over the fence. They didn't hesitate or look back, they just ran. In front of them they could see a silhouette of what appeared to be a vehicle. It was sitting in the middle of the street, with no lights. They heard an engine turn on; it sounded like the old truck they had encountered a while back. The one that had the cloaked ghosts driving the truck.

"Oh fuck, what is that now? It sounds like that old truck that tried to hit us the other day," said Dustin.

"Oh great, that's all we need now. A possessed truck coming after us," said Katrina.

They start to run towards the phantom vehicle, being that is the direction they would need to go to try and get back to their car. The lights turn on, only they aren't normal lights. They are yellow lights, there are circles in the middle of the lights making them now look like yellow glowing eyeballs. The truck revved and revved again. This time, as the engine revved louder than ever, the truck took off at an ungodly speed towards them. So fast, the front end lifted off the ground going into a wheelie as it flies at them with every intention of destruction. The three of them paused for a moment in awe of what they were witnessing. All thinking the same thing, what they are witnessing would be cool if it wasn't trying to bring their eminent death.

Joey grabbed Dustin and Katrina by the arms and pulled them as he ran to the side of the street. The three of them diving behind a large tree, the truck smashed into the other side. The vehicle was going so fast that the whole front end was wrapped around the tree. Joey stood up and walked through the dust that was kicked up and looked in the cab. Nothing, there was no one.

"What the fuck?" said Joey. "I don't think I will ever get used to something like that."

They continue to run. Heading towards Barranca Avenue to head towards the community where their car is parked. Now turning right, they take a peek behind them and now see a bunch of the people that were behind the grenade blasts jumping the fence and sprinting towards them.

"Oh bloody hell. This was a bad idea. Why did we even get involved?" asked Katrina.

Running and now making it close to the train tracks, there comes a slew of people heading through the opening between the walls. They hear a ding-ding-ding, and the train crossing comes down for the street. A train comes flying from the opposing opening and smashes into the crowd while sounding their horn. Their brakes are applied to bring the train to a slow stop. Joey looks down and sees the train crew coming out the front to see what had happened, visually disturbed by the scenario they have encountered, then another person jumps up and grabs him. He never stood a chance, they grabbed him and started smashing his head on the train tracks. There was a second man in the train, he saw what happened to his partner and tried to run the other way, they tripped him, and he fell down, and one guy jumped from the top of the train and slammed his knees on the guy's head. He broke his legs amongst other things, yet the murder of the train crew was the only plan anyway.

"Oh fuck. They just got those guys. Let's hurry up and get to our car," said Joey.

They continued to run as fast as they could. Adrenaline pumping, they are moving faster than they have ever moved in their lives. They get to the entrance of the community and pause to look back and see if there is anyone following them.

"Oh fuck. That is a lot of fucking people coming at us," said Dustin.

They continued to run towards their car. Jumping in and locking the doors, Joey starts the car and throws it in reverse to pull out of the parking spot. Without even trying to be quiet, he slams the pedal down, screeching his tires as he swings back and while still moving throws the shifter to drive. Pushing the gas pedal to the floor, the tires continue to screech as they pick up speed and drive towards the exit. Feeling as if they are about to escape, people are filing out in front of the exit. Not caring, Joey drives right through the wall of the, well whatever they are, zombies, cult members, possessed, who knows what they are.

Joey continues to drive down Foothill Boulevard. going around 80 MPH. Turning on his windshield wipers to hopefully clean the blood splatters off the glass, even though there are now cracks in it from the flying bodies that had bounced off of it.

Then the unexpected happened, red and blue lights flashing in Joey's rear view mirror. They don't know whether to be relieved or to be worried being how all of their police encounters have gone in the past. Joey pulls over the car, puts it in park and rolls down his window.

"How are you doing officer?" said Joey.

"Do you know how fast you were going? Why is there blood on your car?" said the officer.

"Look officer, there is something really crazy going on. We were down at that cemetery hidden off Sierra Madre and there was a lot of people that were..." Joey started to say.

"Have a good night," the officer said while walking away.

Confused about what just happened, Joey looks around, and back to the officer who got into his car and sped off like a bat out of hell.

"Wow, ok. I guess they really do have that much pull with the government. What the fuck do we do now?" asked Joey.

"This is fucking ridiculous. What are we supposed to do?" said Katrina.

After sitting baffled for a few moments, Joey continued to drive home. The roads were empty as to be expected at this time of night. They go back to the garage and go inside.

"Well, I guess we know what happened to Brian after all this time. He's being controlled and is one of them now. I never would've expected that to happen," said Joey.

"He was trying to give us to them. He wanted us to be taken and turned into whatever he was," said Dustin.

"What are we even going to do? It's almost as if we stumbled upon some crazy conspiracy cult who is killing people...Oh wait, that's exactly what we did," said Katrina.

The three of them sat there, just staring at the walls. Not even knowing what to do next. Meanwhile outside, there appears to be fog rolling in.

A large amount of fog, not something usual for this area, or even this time of year.

They continued to run as fast as they could. Adrenaline pumping, they are moving faster than they have ever moved in their lives. They get to the entrance of the community and pause to look back and see if there is anyone following them.

"Oh fuck. That is a lot of fucking people coming at us." Said Dustin.

The continued to run towards their car. Jumping in and locking the doors, Joey starts the car and throws it in reverse to pull out of the parking spot. Without even trying to be quiet, he slams the pedal down screeches his tires as he swings back and while still moving throws the shifter to drive. Pushing the gas pedal to the floor, the tires continue to screech as they pick up speed and drive towards the exit. Feeling as if they are about to escape, people are filing out in front of the exit. Not caring, Joey drives right through the wall of the, well whatever they are, zombies, cult members, possessed, who knows what they are.

Joey continues to drive down Foothill Blvd. going around 80 MPH. Turning on his windshield wipers to hopefully clean the blood splatters off of the glass, even though there are now cracks in it from the flying bodies that were bounced off of it.

Then the unexpected happened, red and blue lights flashing in Joey's rear view mirror. They don't know whether to be relieved or to be worried being how all of their police encounters have gone in the past. Joey pulls over the car, puts it in park, and rolls down his window.

"How are you doing officer?" Said Joey.

"Do you know how fast you were going? Why is there blood on your car?" Said the officer.

"Look officer, there is something really crazy going on. We were down at that cemetery hidden off of Sierra Madre and there was a lot of people that were...." Joey started to say.

"Have a good night." The officer said while walking away.

Confused about what just happened, Joey looks around, and back to the officer who got into his car and sped off like a bat out of hell.

"Wow, ok. I guess they really do have that much pull with the government. What the fuck do we do now?" Asked Joey.

"This is fucking ridiculous. What are we supposed to do?" Said Katrina.

After sitting baffled for a few moments, Joey continued to drive home. The roads were empty as to be expected at this time of night. They get back to the garage and go inside.

"Well, I guess we know what happened to Brian after all this time. He's being controlled and is one of them now. I never would've expected that to happen." Said Joey.

"He was trying to give us to them. He wanted us to be taken and turned into whatever he was." Said Dustin.

"What are we even going to do? It's almost as we stumbled upon some crazy conspiracy cult who is killing people....Oh wait, that's exactly what we did." Said Katrina.

The three of them sat there, just staring at the walls. Not even knowing what to do next. Meanwhile outside, there appears to be fog rolling in. A large amount of fog, not something usual for this area, or even this time of year.

Chapter 18

As they continued to sit and wonder about the madness that they had just witnessed, the fog continued to roll in. It was almost as if someone was controlling the weather and purposely bringing in a dense thick cloud to surround the area. Thinking that they were going to be safe if they stayed there, they decided that it was probably better if they got some sleep. Well, at least try to.

Joey and Katrina lay down in their bed and Dustin laid down on the couch. More than likely, none of them would actually be getting any sleep. They decided they would turn on the TV so that there was some light. They weren't scared of the dark, they were adults. However, with what they just witnessed, it was just safer to have a light source within the room.

After around 20 minutes of sitting in silence, they heard some sort of scratch that came from the front yard. The three of them tensed up simultaneously. Another scratchy noise, and then a thud in what seemed to be in the middle of the street. They all sat up and looked around at each other. There was a scratch now on the garage door, following all the way to the side of the gate. The sound of the gate opening, then the continuing of the scratching on the wall that led to the main door.

BANG BANG BANG.

The door is pounded on repeatedly, fast.

"Oh fuck. They must've followed us here," said Joey.

A familiar voice outside says, "Come outside friends. I am not here to hurt you. I only want to be friends again."

"That's Brian. Of course it's him. What do we do?" said Dustin.

"I don't think he's going to go away. I am going to grab my gun and go outside. I might just have to shoot him. You guys should grab your guns too," said Joey.

Dustin and Katrina nodded in agreement. Joey got up first and grabbed his shotgun, he made his way over to the door. Looking back and seeing they both had their guns as well, standing ready for whatever is to come, he grabs the handle of the door, unlocks it, and kicks open the door. Stepping outside pointing his gun all around to find there is no one there.

"This is really weird guys. Brian is not here, but there is more fog than I've ever seen. I can't even see five feet in front of me," said Joey.

Dustin and Katrina make their way through the door and stand next to Joey.

"Holy fucking shit balls. This is insane," exclaimed Dustin.

"This really can't be good then. Are they controlling the weather now?" asked Katrina.

Though the fog there appeared to be some sort of movement. There were eyes that became visible, almost as if they were glowing. The three of them noticed, all pulled their guns up pointing at the devious eyes. Then there were many, too many sets of eyes to count.

In the distance, Joey heard his brother and parents yelling, "Joey, what was all that banging? I can't see anything through this fog."

Joey turned his head towards the direction of his family's voices.

"Hey, who the fuck are you? What are you doing here? What are you holding...AHHHHHHHHH" screamed Joey's parents.

Joey turned to start running in that direction, but Dustin grabbed him by the arm and pointed behind him. The eyes were now moving towards them. Now full bodies of the many, many coming for them. Katrina fired the first shot at one of them. Dustin and Joey joined and just started to unload as many shots as they could. None of them had extra clips. Click, click.

They had all run out of bullets. They ran back towards the door where they could hopefully get their extra clips, if they had any left. Brian was standing at the door.

"Oh, hey guys. Were you trying to go back to your little safe zone room? Wanting to hide under the covers and hope we would all disappear? Ha ha ha ha. This is real life friends and you guys are fucked."

The three of them had stopped in their tracks looking at Brian, Joey ran straight at him when he heard loud clanks behind him, and he turned his head where he had seen Dustin and Katrina fall from being hit over the head. He turns back around, and Brian is standing in front of him with a steel chair. As if he was a professional wrestler, Brian lifted it above his head and brought it down as hard as he could hitting Joey over the head. The lights go out for Joey.

*****

Starting to open his eyes, Joey's head is throbbing. The lights make it worse. Then he remembers what had just happened. He lifts his head up and sits up to be in some sort of room. It looks like a bedroom, but not one he's ever been in before. There's no furniture, but there are some other bodies lying on the ground. He jumps up hoping those bodies are Katrina, Dustin, and his family. Still concussed, he is dizzy from standing up so fast.

Joey walks over to the first body he sees, its Frank, his brother. He gives him a shake and moves on to the next. Dustin, he shakes him and moves to the next. His parents were together, he shakes them both, looking at his parent,s bloodied faces though, he's sad he has to wake them. Looking around for Katrina now, he panics as he doesn't see any more bodies lying on the ground. There was a grumbling noise above his head. He knew that noise anywhere, Katrina was suspended from the ceiling with small ropes tied to her wrists and ankles.

"Oh shit! Katrina! We need to get her down guys. Does anyone have a knife or anything that could cut the ropes?" Joey panicked.

They all checked their pockets and shook their heads no.

"Dustin, put me on your shoulders and take me to the corner of the rope. I am going to pull it out of the ceiling. One at a time. Frank, stand below Katrina and try to hold her up some so there's not so much tension on her where the rope is tied."

Dustin walked over to Joey and put him on his shoulders. The first rope he is trying to pull out is attached to Katrinas right ankle. Joey grabs the rope and pulls with all his might. It didn't budge. Joey grabbed with two hands and leaned back, Dustin went off balance and fell backwards, too. They both crashed to the ground; however, it worked, and the rope was out of the ceiling. They repeated this three more times, each time ended with them falling to the ground. Joey was hurting extra now that he fell four times, but this did not faze him as he got up and ran to Katrina.

"Are you ok? I am going to kill Brian for this. He led them to us. I am going to kill them all!" said Joey.

Katrina was rubbing the marks on her wrists, "I am ok, I guess. A lot better now that I am down. Where are we?"

"I have no idea where we are. I woke up and saw us all here laying down," said Joey.

The lights turned off; a red flashing light turned on. There was banging on all four walls. Fast and repeated banging, louder and louder. The door lock released, and the door slowly crept open. The banging subsided. They made their way cautiously to the door. Joey peaked out and looked in both directions.

"The coast is clear. It's an empty hallway. Left or right?" asked Joey.

Everyone looked at each other, not really knowing which way to go, Dustin pointed left.

"Left it is," said Joey.

He started to lead them out, one by one they followed in slow quiet steps. Joey reaches the end of the hallway, there is only one direction to turn, right. He peaks his head around and sees that there is nothing there as well, just another dark hallway. Joey shrugs and continues down the hallway. Once they get halfway down the hallway, Joey hears a noise in the back and turns around to look. There, he sees two large men wearing leather masks with only the eyes cut out and a zipper on the mouth, leather pants, and leather gloves. They have a hold of Joey's dad.

Joey's father yells, "Run! Get everyone out of here son."

Joey screams, "NOOOOOOOOOOOOOO!"

One of the men stab his father in the stomach with a very large blade, repeatedly. The other was holding a hatchet, in which he swung it around and hit him square in the face. His blood sprayed everywhere as his body convulsed and fell to the ground.

Joey's mother screams, Frank grabbed her by the arm, and they all ran. Joey leading the way ran throughout the house and saw a door. It appeared to be a sliding glass door that led to the backyard. There were many people in the back, all wearing cloaks. He stopped and turned around running back in the other direction. This led to another room, however just as he was going to reach there, two men stepped out of the hallway. Joey, not being too far from where they were, and being as mad as he was, yelled at the top of his lungs sounding like a Viking doing a battle cry. Joey jumped at them, aiming his head at one of their faces and elbowing the other in the face as the three of them collided.

Joey knocked both of them out cold, he stood up and started to stomp their faces repeatedly. Dustin ran up and kicked the lifeless bodies in the nuts. Katrina grabbed Joey and guided him to keep moving. Frank kicked them as he went by their now bloodied bodies on the ground. Joey found the front door. Locked. He stood back and kicked right by the handle repeatedly until the door swung open. The door was definitely reinforced, as it took many kicks to open the door. Joey ran out of the house, realizing where they were, the cult house by the cemetery.

"Holy. Fucking. Shit," Joey said, as he stood still looking in front of him.

As the rest of them piled out and nearly ran right into Joey, they stopped right behind him noticing what it was he was staring at. Two rows of people in cloaks, holding torches. Making it so there is only one way for them to go, right down the middle of them; and it leads to the cemetery.

"I guess we don't have any other option than to go through there. Fuck," said Joey.

They slowly walk down the path, as they pass the cloaked people, the entrance behind them closes. Every set of people they pass, they continue to grow behind them. This raises the fear and they start to move a little faster. Finally making it to the entrance of the cemetery, there is an altar in the middle surrounded by large pillars flaming at the top. There are two people standing next to the alter.

They wear different cloaks then everyone else, something that seems to have more importance somehow. These are a darker red, with gold symbols and designs. Still walking slowly, not really wanting to know what's going to happen when they get to the altar, the group is now being pushed. One of the normal cloaked people steps up next to them and pulls their hood down. It's Brian.

"You mother fucker! You set us up!" yelled Joey.

Dustin yelled, then ran up directly to Brian. He kicked him right between the legs, making Brian fall to the ground. Dustin managed to get one more kick directly to Brians face. This knocked him unconscious. Dustin was then tackled by three of the cloaked men. The rest of the group was now grabbed from all angles and held in place while waiting for directions from their leaders. The leader pointed towards Joey's mother in which the ones holding her brought her to the altar.

"I could only imagine what you guys must be thinking. What are these people doing here? Well, here's the thing, we run everything behind closed doors. We are everywhere. We follow the Dark Lord himself. We make sacrifices to him, he gives us control over certain demons, and spirits. Today, you will all make great sacrifices for us. You had to keep poking into our business, so now you have our attention and will be a part of our business," said the leader.

He pointed to the altar in which Joey's mother was forced to lay her head over. There was a chalice underneath her, with a pentagram engraved on the side. The leader then pulled out a dagger, Damascus steel. He proceeded to bring it to Joey's mother's throat and sliced, blood sprayed everywhere while her body convulsed, even though still being suspended by everyone holding her.

Joey, Frank, Dustin, Katrina stands and stare in shock. They couldn't even make any sounds or reactions. Joey's and Frank's parents were now both dead. In a short period of time, although adults, Joey and Frank became orphans.

"Joey, mom and dad are dead. What the fuck are we going to do?" asked Frank.

"I don't know," Joey answered, while still in shock.

The leader then pointed to Frank. Knowing what this now means, Frank starts to yell and tried to turn around, but he was taken to the man. He then licks the blood-soaked blade, slicing him on his back. This time, he isn't going for a quick kill, he is slicing and dicing his way through Frank's flesh. Frank is screaming as filets of skin are being removed and thrown into the crowd of people. Some of them being smacked in the face by it, only to quickly remove it and eat it as if they have never eaten before and were being fed a McDonald's filet o' fish, only this is a filet o' Frank.

Frank passes out from the pain; Joey drops to his knees. Dustin and Katrina don't know what to do, so they continue to just stand there unresponsive. Joey's entire family has now been slaughtered in front of him. All within a few hours. The leader grabbed the chalice and took a sip from the blood-ridden drink. He handed it to the other person with the same cloak who hadn't been doing anything without being told what to do. He then takes a drink and hands it back. The leader proceeds to dip his finger into the blood and starts painting symbols on his own forehead. He spins the chalice spraying the blood on everyone that is near them, including what's left of The Spirit Brigade.

The leader then points to Joey, in which they drag him to the altar. Joey, not willing to stand up, hold him up.

"I've got something special for you boy," the leader said to Joey.

He then starts to chant and speak in some language that none of them could figure out what it was. There was a part in the cloaked disciples. That's when they saw the truck door open. It looked exactly like the haunted truck that crashed. The cloak that is not inhabited by a body suddenly fills out after being flat on the driver seat. The invisible being steps out of the truck and starts to make its way towards them.

"Oh fuck," was the only thing Joey could say.

As the hovering cloak is about ten feet away from Joey, there is a sudden noise from a distance. This doesn't bother the being, but everyone else turns their heads as they hear a police siren making its way towards them.

"I thought we owned the police," the leader said to his second in command.

"We do. I don't possibly know what this could be about," said the disciple.

The police car with its lights and sirens come around and into view from Sierra Madre. The entity is now five feet from Joey. The police car turns onto the dirt and starts plowing through the crowd of followers. Joey then regains strength, knowing he still has a girlfriend and friend to protect. He headbutts the nose of one of the people holding him. Then turns and kicks the other in the nuts. Grabbing the blade off the altar, he then plunges it directly into the leader's eye. He pulls it out and stabs him in the throat. He then repeatedly stabs him in the face and chest until it looks like he was hit with an open blender.

Joey looks back at the monster that was stalking him, only to find that the cloak was now just a pile of dirty laundry.

"Well, lookie here. It appears you guys do have vulnerabilities," said Joey.

Although this does feel like a win, there is still the fact that they are surrounded by the followers, and Joey had just killed their leader. The police officer that had just plowed through a bunch of them had made his way to the altar. There were too many bodies that had collected underneath his police cruiser. He opened the door; it turned out to be the police chief.

"I couldn't let you do it on your own. I knew what was going on was wrong. It wasn't until you came and saw me that I realized that I needed to help get rid of the problem. I shouldn't have ever been involved and let it happen," the police chief yelled.

As soon as he was done yelling to the group, the bodies that were surrounding the car started to get up. They grabbed him, pulled him to the ground. Yelling and screaming of agony commenced. All Joey, Dustin, and Katrina could see was blood and what appeared to be flaps of flesh flying everywhere. Joey jumped up and grabbed Katrina and Dustin, but the arms and continued to run towards the previously possessed truck.

The followers were too occupied with the police officer to notice that they were running away. They reached the truck, Joey jumped into the driver seat, Katrina in the middle and Dustin in the passenger seat. The truck was already running, Joey hit the gas and peeled out away from the carnage. Joey drove about two miles away when he went past Goddard Middle School. Joey pulled over, looked over at Dustin and Katrina, all still in shock.

"What should we do? How the fuck do we fix this? I already killed their leader, but how do we get rid of all of it?" asked Joey.

"Kill them all," said Katrina. "Let's blow up the farmhouse."

"Actually, that might just be the way to do it. But how do we do that right now? We should also destroy that altar," said Dustin.

"Let's get a shit ton of gasoline. Fill up gallons of bottles and drive this truck directly into the house. After that let's run to the altar and destroy it," answered Joey.

Katrina and Dustin nodded in agreement.

Chapter 19

Joey drove them to the gas station where they bought ten gallons of water. They drank some of it, then poured the rest of it out on the ground outside. They proceeded to fill up all the gallon bottles with gasoline. Every time they filled one of them up, they put it in the truck bed. After all ten gallons were filled up and they were happy to have at least that amount of gasoline, they put the pump back onto its station.

Joey then drove back by his house where he knew he had two sledgehammers that would suffice for destroying the altar. After getting the hammers, he continued to drive back to the farmhouse off Sierra Madre. Joey got to the long driveway of the farmhouse. He pulled in and put the truck into park.

"Ok guys, hopefully when this truck slams into the house and blows up, all of the people at the cemetery will run back and we can destroy that altar," said Joey.

Everyone jumped out of the truck, Joey aimed the steering wheel so it would go directly into the front door of the farmhouse. Joey looked around and didn't see anything that could hold the gas pedal down, so he reached into the truck bed and grabbed one of the gallons of gasoline. Joey then laid it down so the gas pedal was being pushed. As the engine revved, Joey reached over and shifted the gear into drive. The truck peeled out and flew towards the farmhouse.

There were some of the followers near the front of the farmhouse. They ran in front of the truck trying to deter it from hitting the house. All that did was hit them and make one of them fly back towards the house and bounce off the wall, the other was pulled under the tire. The truck then slammed into the house and exploded beyond what they imagined would happen.

The middle of the house erupted into flames. Immediately, fire sprung from the front and back of the farmhouse. This caused the commotion that they had hoped would happen. All the people at the cemetery started to run towards the farmhouse frantically. Joey, Dustin, and Katrina ran towards the cemetery, going the long way so they would stay unseen. They reached the cemetery noticing that not everyone had left. There were still two people by the altar. The second in command, who would probably now be in charge, and Brian.

"We have some unfinished business," Brian said, while looking at Dustin.

Brian took off running at Dustin and punched him in the face. Dustin once again kicked him right in the nuts. He then kicked him three more times in the nuts before he fell to the ground. Screaming, Brian grabbed a stick off the ground and stabbed it through Dustin's leg. Dustin yelled in agony, but remembering he had a sledgehammer, lifted it and slammed it down onto Brian's face. Brian instantly went limp. Dustin repeatedly lifted and slammed the hammer onto Brian's face. There was nothing left of Brian's head as Dustin's hammer hit the dirt behind Brian's head.

The body started to convulse and there was blood everywhere. Joey looked at the other man at the altar who was still staring at Dustin in disbelief.

"I guess we should've tried to get you instead," the man said in Dustin's direction.

Joey ran up and elbowed him in the face. The man fell to the ground, Joey jumped on top of him sitting in full mount. He then repeatedly drove down what he would like to call hell bows to the man's head. The man's face now looked as if he was being pulverized by the hammer. Joey was satisfied and got off the limp body. He then walked over and grabbed the hammer and hit the body. He didn't start at the head though; he wanted to make sure he suffered if he was still alive. He started hitting his feet, then shins, and so on and so on till he reached his head. After Joey was done, the body might as well as been a pile of slime.

"Let's destroy this shit," Joey yelled to Dustin and Katrina.

They looked to the altar and started to hit it with the hammers. Pieces of the stone altar started to fall off. There were sparks flying as it was hit. Clouds started to roll in and rain started to fall. There was never any rain in sight until they started to hit the altar. Every hit, there was lightning and thunder. Spirits started to release as they were hitting it.

Katrina looked around, "Uh...Joey. Look. There is a bunch of spirits surrounding us now."

Joey and Dustin stopped and looked around. There were tons of spirits inhabiting the cemetery. Joey's parents and brother were among the spirits.

"Please, destroy this thing. Once it is broken, we will finally be at peace," a spirit said.

The spirit looked as if it might have been from the 1800s. Joey, feeling empathy for the spirit nodded as a tear fell from his eye once he noticed his family. Joey and Dustin continued to slam the hammers into the altar when they noticed that the followers were starting to make their way into the cemetery. Running towards them, screaming, the spirits turned towards them as they piled in. The spirits started to attack all of them holding them back.

Dustin and Joey screamed as they both slammed the hammers down next to each other and the altar split. One last smack from both of them and lightning sprung out of the altar into the sky. The altar split into two with orange glowing from the stone. The altar turned into a melting lava substance and dissipated into the ground.

The followers that were trying to run in stopped running. The spirits all turned to Dustin and Joey, they then disappeared and faded away.

"I think you just set them free," Katrina said.

The followers were shaking their heads as if they had just woken up from a bad dream and were looking around at each other.

"Where am I? What am I doing here?" said one of the followers.

The remainder of them, all confused, started to walk away. They were most likely trying to walk back to their homes, if they still had one. Lights and sirens started flying down the road of Sierra Madre. They all came flying in the side where the deceased police chief's vehicle was. Jumping out of their vehicles with guns drawn, they inspected the police chief's vehicle. Joey started approaching the policemen with his hands up.

"Hey guys, I know who you're looking for. He was killed. He saved us though, and in saving us we were able to stop all of them. Did you guys know what was going on?" Joey asked.

"Unfortunately, yes, we did. Now, you three need to get out of here. Being that it was a cult doing all of these crazy things, the FBI was called, and they are making their way here. Hurry and go. Thank you. You don't know what you did for the world, let alone just our town," said a police officer.

Joey, Dustin, and Katrina started walking towards the garage. The place where all of this started for them. This was a good distance of a walk for them; however, they didn't care about the walk. All of them were beat up, limping, and hurt. After a long and quiet walk, they made it to their garage where they went inside and laid down and instantly fell asleep.

Chapter 20

The three of them woke up, sat up, looked around and realized that this was still their reality. They turned on the TV, every channel had the news showing the FBI going through the farmhouse, or what was left of it after the fire department put out the fire. They had the identities of the leader and all of the bodies that were found within the cemetery. They started to list the names that were sacrificed, as well as connecting many of their escapades that this cult had caused. So many disasters, so many deaths.

This was now being listed as the most devastating and diabolical group that has ever been seen. Joey's family was now being shown as victims, the three of them dropped their heads in sadness.

"I can't believe they are gone. In one whole fucking day my whole family was murdered," said Joey.

"I am so sorry brother. I really hope you can heal over time," Dustin said.

Katrina hugged Joey and squeezed him tightly. They all took turns taking showers so they could get some type of relief. Now they realized that they were hungry, ordering pizza so they didn't have to do anything. There was a knock on the garage door. Joey got to the door and opened it.

"Hi, I am looking for Joey, Dustin, and Katrina. Is that you three?" said a man dressed in black.

"Yes. Who are you?" answered Joey.

"I am an FBI agent. For undisclosed reasons, I am not giving my name but just know that the United States government appreciates what you have done. We will make sure that your family's deaths do not go unnoticed and that they are honored for helping. You will all be rewarded a good sum of money but do know that this can never be spoken of to anyone. It is important that the official story that goes out in the media stays the same. So just know, by taking this money, which will make it so you never have to work again, you will be signing a contract, NDA."

"Well fuck. That sounds good to me. How about you guys?" Joey said to Dustin and Katrina, who both nodded yes, "Looks like we all agree."

"Well then, it's settled. Within 24 hours, three contracts will be delivered for you to sign. Once you do, there will be deposits in your accounts. This will all be over with. One last thing, I am sorry for your losses."

Over the next few weeks, the city started to rebuild. A new police chief was appointed, and the farmhouse was torn down. Everything started to shift back into normal-ish. The three of them were now well off and hung out just as much as they did before. The only difference, they were no longer trying to find wild situations to get themselves into. In fact, they were happy to keep the mundane and boring nights. They have had enough excitement to last a lifetime.

The End.

Also by

Short Stories: Tales of Madness
New Witch in Town

About the author

Michael Gregory II is the author's name at birth, but generally goes by Mike. Growing up,

Mike enjoyed being a storyteller to family and friends. As a young child, Mike used his mother's electric typewriter to write short stories and shared them with his grandmother. Mike began writing short stories for fun and found that it was a true passion for him. He has always loved books, movies, or even just a well-told story. Mike is enjoying the journey of sharing his passion with others.

If you would like to connect with him. You can find him on:
Twitter.com/**mikegreg85**
Instagram.com/mikegreg85
Facebook.com/mikegregory85
Website: www.mg-books.com

Please add a short review on Amazon/Goodreads and let me know what you thought of this book!

www.ingramcontent.com/pod-product-compliance
Lightning Source LLC
LaVergne TN
LVHW041756060526
838201LV00046B/1019